In Too Hard

He came around to my side of the desk and leaned against the front, facing me, offering me the box. "This is for you."

"It is?" I said, looking at the box like it might be a trap of some sort. We'd just come to an alliance about my continued working for him. Then to throw a gift into things? On Valentine's Day? "What is it?" I asked, still not reaching for it.

He leaned forward and placed the box on my lap. I almost opened my knees and shut them, catching his hand, like it was the *Pretty Woman* pearls. Oh, to have his hand between my legs.

But I was neither quick nor brave enough to pull it off, and he placed the box without touching me at all.

"Open it," he answered, giving me no clue as to its contents.

"But, why?" I asked, then began unwrapping it, sticking the bow to the arm of my chair.

"I got it for you in Gstaad. I'd intended on giving it to you that first day I got back, I even had it in my bag. But I got…distracted."

I looked up at him and raised a brow, knowing full well what had distracted him. My mouth. My body. My kisses.

He cleared his throat before continuing, but I did notice his gaze had dropped to my mouth. "Anyway. Instead of a holiday gift, I guess it has become a peace offering of sorts."

"But…today?"

"Why not today?" he asked.

I looked at him questioningly, but he just shrugged, not knowing what I was getting at. Sighing, I said, "Because it's Valentine's Day?"

The look on his face was classic Absent-Minded Professor. "Aw, shit," he said.

I lowered my gaze and continued to slowly unwrap the box, the thrill somewhat tarnished knowing that he hadn't meant anything romantic by his gift-giving timing. My hands were sure, though my emotions weren't, as I slid the wrapping paper from the box, which had some French name on the cover embossed in gold.

He sighed. Suddenly he was on his haunches in front of me, his hands stilling mine, sliding under them, so that our palms met.

I stared at our joined hands, until he laced his fingers with my willing ones, then I looked up into his grey gaze. His eyes weren't the stormy seas, but that of a crisp, cold winter sky.

"Syd, will you be my Valentine?" he whispered.

IN TOO
HARD

Freshman Roommates, Book Three

MARA JACOBS

Published by Copper Country Press, LLC
©Copyright 2015 Mara Jacobs
Cover design by Mara Jacobs

ISBN: 978-1-940993-80-5

For more information on the author and her works, please
see www.marajacobs.com

For Every Great
Forbidden Love
Romance

ONE

I was in love with Billy Montrose for five years.
And then I met him.

"Ms. O'Brien and Ms. Winters, would you both please stay after for a moment?" Professor Montrose said to my suitemate Jane and me as our class was dismissing. For the final time. We were a day away from semester break.

He wasn't really a professor. He was a guest instructor for this year only—the year I was a freshman at Bribury College. The elite, Ivy League Lite college that I'd busted my ass to get into with a scholarship.

I didn't belong here, but I tried like hell not to let it show.

The rest of the class filed out, some looking back with curiosity, some just happy to begin their winter break.

Lily Spaulding, our third suitemate, gave us both a nod as she left, but she didn't wait. Probably off to meet her boyfriend Lucas. They'd recently been reunited and Lily had basically been walking on a cloud ever since.

Besides the nod in both our directions, Lily'd given Jane a stern, warning look. I guessed she feared Jane would make a pass at Montrose while given the opportunity of a private audience.

I was afraid of that too, and not just because I'd be in the room to witness it.

I had basically held my breath all semester long hoping that Montrose wouldn't succumb to Jane's blatant innuendoes and outrageous flirting.

He hadn't. But now, as of today actually, Jane was no longer his student. And if that had been the ethical barrier holding him back, it was now lifted.

"Ms. Winters, you first, please," Montrose said, half-leaning, half-sitting against the side of his desk.

A perturbed look crossed Jane's face. She knew what I'd just figured out—Montrose wouldn't ask to speak with her first if he was going to relent to her pursuit. Not with me in the room.

Trying to give them some privacy, I stepped away from the seats we'd all vacated before he'd asked for Jane and me to stay. I walked to the other side of the room so I wouldn't hear what they said, though I desperately wanted to. I moved to where I could see Jane's face and Montrose's back.

Even his back was gorgeous.

He wasn't handsome in the traditional way, and certainly not pretty, like so many of the privileged Bribury boys. But there was just something about him that screamed sexy. His hair was dark brown and worn a little long, but not nearly as long as Lily's Lucas wore his. Not down to his shoulders, but more like he'd missed his last two haircut appointments.

He always looked tired, and was almost always late for class even though it wasn't a crack o' dawn start time.

He wore jeans most of the time, occasionally khaki cargo pants. Even though he usually paired it with a sports coat and tie, he always looked a little disheveled and sometimes even disoriented.

But when he lectured, you could see, hear and feel the

intelligence he possessed.

Though he taught Intro to Creative Writing, he almost always brought his favorite literature into each lecture. How Hemingway did this. How Wolfe did that. Or Woolf. He was keen on both.

Being a voracious reader since I'd been fourteen, I ate it all up, taking notes on his favorite, but obscure, authors. Knowing I'd be able to finally read for pleasure once the semester was over, I added them all to my growing To Be Read author list.

Montrose was twenty-eight, and had written *Gangster's Folly*, which had been touted as the Great American Novel, when he was twenty-three.

I don't know if it truly was *the* Great American Novel.

But it was the novel that saved my life.

Now I watched Jane's face and could tell he wasn't hitting on her. Not by the look of "fuck you" that she was silently giving him. He reached out and placed a hand on her shoulder and I held my breath for a second until his hand dropped away from her.

Jane's look softened. I barely heard the murmur of what he said next, not able to make out any of the words. He gestured to the paper she held in her hand. The paper we'd gotten back from Montrose today. Our final paper, weighted at half our grade. We were supposed to start with "The person I am today is…" then write.

I held my own in my hand—I'd been about to put it in my backpack when Montrose had asked us to stay.

I'd scored a ninety-seven on it and saw a bunch of comments, which I would read the second I was alone.

Jane looked at Montrose for a long while after he'd finished speaking, and then she gave a tiny nod of her head and just a hint of a smile.

Not the flirty smile I'd seen her use on him before. The

smile that said she was a very naughty girl and needed teacher to discipline her.

And not the smile that she gave to people just before she sliced them a new vein with her sharp words.

It was a smile that perhaps only Lily and I ever saw.

And now Montrose.

My heart fell to my stomach. They'd reached some kind of...truce, I guessed. Would there be more?

I knew Montrose was out of my league, that I could never make myself flirt with him, having idolized him for five years.

But that didn't mean I wanted Jane to be with him.

She gave him a playful punch on the arm and turned and walked away. "See ya back at the room later, Syd," she said, not turning around, but waving a hand to me over her shoulder as she slipped her coat on.

"See ya," I said to her back as I made my way over to my seat.

I looked to Montrose who turned his attention from Jane leaving back to me. "Now, Ms. O'Brien," he said, "your turn."

TWO

"DID YOU WANT to talk about this?" I said to Montrose, holding up my paper.

"No. I mean, that's not why I asked you to stay. But if you want to talk about it, that's fine."

I shook my head. "No, I'm happy with my grade."

"You should be. It was the highest in the class. All sections of the class."

That fact made me extremely happy, but I didn't let it show. I didn't want anyone to know how badly I wanted to do better than these rich kids.

"So, not the paper?" I said, putting it in my backpack, then turning back to him.

He moved around to the front of the desk and leaned against it, crossing his legs at the ankles. Putting his hands behind him on the desk he stared at me. Sort of. His focus was on me, but he had kind of a far off gaze, like he sometimes got during class, before he got rolling.

He did an actual shake of his head, like he was trying to get rid of the cobwebs. "Sorry. Umm…"

"Why you asked me to stay?" I said, trying to remind him.

"Right. Right. Well, they've added another section of my class for next semester. Which I didn't take very well. There are a *lot* of papers to read for this class."

"Yes, I know. It was a lot of papers to write."

He smiled a little. "You managed it, though, right? Even with your other classes, and working in the admin building?"

"How did you know I worked there?"

"You mentioned it in one of your papers."

"I did?" I didn't remember that.

"Something about how you likened working in the admin building with being an Orwellian character."

I barely remembered writing that, but he, who read how many student papers this semester, pulled it out of his—seemingly—far-away brain.

"Oh, right. Yeah, I forgot."

He looked dead on at me, his gaze for once focused and, I have to admit, a bit disarming. "I didn't forget. It was a great line. Very fitting, very visual."

"Only if you'd read *Animal Farm*."

He tilted his head a little, still staring at me with startling grey eyes. "But I *have* read it. And I'm guessing you knew that, right?"

I shrugged. "I assumed." I didn't bring up that he'd mentioned *Animal Farm* being very important to him in one of the many interviews he'd done post *Folly* hitting it big. No need for him to think I was a book stalker or anything.

Because I wasn't. Well, not totally.

He nodded. "Good assumption." Then he shook his head again, and his look softened, almost went out of focus. "Anyway. So, you were able to keep up with classes and a job in the admin building this semester? No issues?"

I shook my head a little bit, not really sure where this was going. "No issues. I have to have the job as part of my scholarship stipulations, and I have to maintain a 3.25 GPA."

"And you will?"

"Should be a 3.7 or around there."

He smiled softly, and just a hint of his perfectly straight, white teeth showed. "What? No four-point-oh?"

"I had a blip in Calculus."

"God, just a blip? I flunked Calc. I think twice." The smile again, this time a little bigger.

It was all I could do not to pull my top off and rub myself all over him. I tucked a strand of my straight hair behind an ear—a nervous habit I was trying to break. Like all my bad habits that I'd brought to Bribury. "But, anyway…yes, I was able to handle both the job and grades. It wasn't a lot of hours at the admin building."

"Think you could handle more?"

It wasn't a loaded question in any way. No sexual innuendo in his voice at all. And yet I very much wanted to channel Jane and give him a Mae West answer about what all I could handle. "Yes," was all I said.

"Good. I have something I think you'd be great at. It's not for credits—though it should be—and it isn't part of a work/study program, so you'd still have to keep your job at the admin building."

He paused, and I nodded, waiting for him to go on.

"I balked at the extra section. Loudly. Part of the reason I took this year away from the city to do this was so I could really buckle down on my next novel. I barely got a few ideas jotted down this semester, and I jot down a *lot* of notes. I can only imagine the extra time it will take this spring."

"Can't they give you a TA or something, to help with reading all the papers?"

I briefly wondered if that's what he had in mind for me. But no. They wouldn't let a freshman, who had only just had the one class on creative writing, wield that much power over her fellow freshmen's papers.

"They did offer a TA. And I probably should have taken

it. But…I *really* like reading all the papers. Giving comments. Seeing if any of the stuff we talked about in class got through. I didn't want to give that up. Not entirely. But then, what? Half the students have their papers read and critiqued by me, and the other half by a TA? That didn't seem right. And, well, I'm sure a lot of people just randomly got my class. But, I'd like to think a few had actually heard of me and wanted to take the class *because* of me. So it didn't seem, I don't know, *right* to not read the papers myself."

I wanted to tell him I'd taken his class because of him. That every time we had a paper returned I'd read and reread his comments on them. I just nodded and said, "Yes, I can see that. I think it's good you want to read them yourself."

"Is it?" He ran his hand across his mouth. A beautiful mouth with full lips, the lower one looking particularly suck-worthy. "Yeah. Good. I thought so.

"So instead of taking on a TA, they gave me the funds to use for an administrative assistant."

"But if they wouldn't be helping with the papers, or the class, what would the assistant be doing for you?" I asked. Then I had a vision of me running around town picking up Montrose's dry cleaning and doing his grocery shopping or something.

I hated chores. With a passion. I'd had to do all of that back home, with two baby brothers and a mother that was, at best, neglectful, at worst, MIA.

And a father who, at least for me, was never in the picture.

Coming to Bribury, living in the dorms, meant I didn't have to do those mundane chores anymore.

Sure, I had to do my laundry, and hit the store for snacks to have in the room and stuff like that. But I wasn't planning dinner, or making sure the boys got to bed. Or to preschool. Or, basically survived.

So, the freedom of that kind of chore was symbolic to me, and I didn't want to look back.

But the idea of being in Montrose's life, even if it was to water his plants or something, was *very* tempting.

"Laundry, groceries, that type of thing?" I asked. I was about to nod my head that I'd be interested, but was stopped by his head shaking and the holding up of his hands.

"No. No. Nothing like that. I have a cleaning person who does all that crap."

"Oh. What then?" Maybe my Mae West comeback wouldn't have been far off base after all. Maybe he was looking for a different sort of "help."

He motioned to my vacated chair for me to sit, which I did. Then he sat in Jane's empty seat, turning his body toward mine. "For a long time now, I've been writing my second novel."

"Okay?"

He rubbed his chin again, a look that was so "introspective professor" but on a young, hot face.

"Well, actually, not so much *writing* my next novel, as *working* on it. More like jotting down lots of notes on several different ideas I'm toying with."

"I'm assuming that's just part of the writing process?"

He shrugged, and looked forward, to the front of the classroom. He seemed kind of surprised by the role reversal, looking at the desk that he often leaned on as he lectured.

"I guess," he said. "I don't really know what the writing process is. Or what *my* typical process is. *Folly* just poured out of me. No notes, nothing. It was just a story I had to tell. This one…has not been…effortless."

"Well, no. I imagine most novels aren't. You'll probably never have the experience you had with *Folly* again."

His shoulders slumped, and he put his elbows on the little half table part of the desk. "That is the conclusion I have come to." He looked over at me with an embarrassed smile. "And it took me five years to figure that out."

"Better late than never?" I lamely offered.

"Yeah, I suppose."

"I mean, it's not like you've passed your prime. You're still only…" I checked myself. "Late twenties? You haven't even hit thirty yet, have you?"

He'd turned twenty-eight on October third. Unfortunately a day I didn't have his class. Not that I would have brought it up or anything, but I thought maybe somebody in the class would have seen it online or somewhere and said something.

"Nope, not thirty. Only twenty-eight." He looked to the ceiling. "God. Thirty in two fucking years."

"It's not exactly seventy."

He shook his head and laughed a little, then looked at me. "You're right. This might be a good arrangement. Don't let me wallow, Ms. O'Brien. I tend to be a bit of a self-entitled prick at times."

"Then you're in the right place," I said, waving my arms, encompassing all things Bribury.

An actual, full-bodied, laugh came out of him. A rich, deep sound that made my breath catch just a tiny bit, though I was very careful not to show my reaction.

"Yeah, pretty much," he said. "So, I need to get my notes together. I've been rather…lax these past five years in organizing them in any way."

"Are they all electronic? On your laptop or something?"

"Hardly any of them. And there are boxes and boxes. I had them all shipped to the apartment the college provided for me for the year. I sublet my place in New York, so I wanted them all here. Plus, I thought I'd have lots of time to work with them."

"And you haven't because of the class. I get it."

"Well, yeah. But, if I'm honest, every time I open one of the boxes to get started on it, it all feels, I don't know, daunting or something. And I panic and shut the boxes up.

"I even brought a few of them to my office in this building, thinking maybe that would help."

"And it didn't?"

He shook his head. "Nope." He turned his whole body to face me, the slope of the desk lifting the flap of his sports coat, showing off his white, cotton oxford beneath. "What I'm looking for is someone to go through all the boxes, organize the notes by the different novel ideas, and then transcribe them all into an outline format for each of the books."

"Books? Plural?"

"Oh, God, there must be ideas for twenty different novels in all those boxes."

I was already nodding, going into organizational mode. "Can you give me your top three or four book ideas that will have the most notes? Maybe the priority I should use when working through them?"

His eyes, light grey earlier, turned a deeper shade as an almost tortured look crossed his face. "That's just it. There is no front-runner. Or top three or four. It's just all one big jumbled mess of ideas. I can't...I haven't been able to..."

I wanted to reach out and touch his arm, to soothe him. It was obvious that he was in some kind of literary pain. But sympathy—and touching—probably wouldn't help me get the job.

Which made me wonder... "Why did you ask me? I mean, I'm assuming you're asking me if I'd be interested in the job?"

"I am. The job's yours if you want it." His face cleared of the clouds a little, and he looked at me with a bit of searching.

"I do. But again, why me? Not that I don't think I'd be good at it. I do. I think it'd be right up my alley, actually."

"So do I. That's why I came to you. As to why I picked you? Well, you referenced a lot of literature in your papers, so it's obvious you're well-read." I nodded and waited. "From the paper you wrote about where you came from, it's apparent that, let's say, organizational skills were a part of your daily life."

A nice way of saying I had to hold it all together because no one else would. "Yes, I'm very organized."

He nodded, but his look said he knew more about me than I wanted him to, that he'd read between the lines. A necessary evil, I supposed, if you're going to be truthful in your writing class.

"Well, this job is going to take a lot of organizing. And from the way you wrote your papers, it was obvious you understand basic literary structure. That will be key when you're transcribing the notes into a workable outline."

"Makes sense."

He leaned a little closer. Not quite in my space, but a little past his. "But the kicker was when you wrote about one of your favorite hobbies—besides reading—being jigsaw puzzles."

"You remember *that?*"

He smiled. "I do."

"And that was beneficial to this?" I motioned between him and me, then waved it around the classroom for good measure.

"Yes. It was like a light bulb went off for me when I was given the okay for an assistant. Because this is going to be one big, gigantic, friggin' jigsaw puzzle."

To do something I would truly love, and to do it in the Billy Montrose atmosphere? "Yes. I would really like to do this."

"You don't even want to know what it pays?"

And to get *paid* to do it? But I put on my poker face. "Well, yes. What would the pay be? What hours would you need me? I don't have a car on campus, would that be an issue?"

He settled back in his chair, but still faced me. Did I

imagine it, or did he let out a tiny sigh of relief? "The hours are whenever you're available. It's a lump sum for the job, paid out at the beginning of each month starting in January and going through May. It's not an hourly wage, but for the completed job, so you can work whenever you're able. I'll get you a key to my office. And once you're through there we'll figure out what to do with the boxes in my apartment. It's right on the edge of campus, and I walk it, but maybe we'd bring all the boxes down to the office. Or we…I don't know, we'll figure it out, okay?"

"Okay."

"The total for the job is ten thousand dollars. They figured it at their starting administrative assistant's rate for six months. I can disperse that as I see fit. You're obviously not expected to work forty hours, but you only have five months to do the job.

"You'd be paid two thousand on the first of each month. We would be in constant contact, obviously, with your progress. If it doesn't seem like you can finish it all before you're done for the year—"

"I'll get it done." Holy shit. Ten thousand would be a huge help with my expenses. It would maybe even allow me to stay here over the summer and get a few classes in.

The thought of going home for the summer had been the only sense of dread I'd had since arriving at Bribury.

He smiled. "Ms. O'Brien, you have not seen the amount of notes we're talking about."

"I'll get it done. I accept the offer."

"Great." He stood up and moved to his desk and started to shove things into his satchel. "Are you still on campus tomorrow, or are you heading home today?"

"No, I'm here tomorrow. Actually, I'm staying through the break. Because of my job with the admin building, I'm helping with the testing of the new front end system they're installing over the break."

"Oh, yeah," he said, turning around. "I remember reading about that. A big deal, I guess?"

"Yeah. It affects every system on campus."

"Right, right. I have to do something different for online grading next semester or…something. I have the email on it."

"Yes. So, I'm here through the whole break."

"Not going home at all?" he asked. He'd finished packing his bag, grabbed his coat and came to stand in front of me.

I stood up and reached for my coat. He took it from my hands and held it open for me. The gesture was so foreign to me that it took me a second to realize he was helping me. If that had happened in my neighborhood, the guy would have taken off running, my coat in hand, and me chasing after him.

I slid into the coat, wishing his hands would linger on my shoulders or some such mushy crap, but he stepped away as soon as the garment was on.

"No. No plans to go home. The pay for doing the testing over the holidays is too good to pass up." I turned to face him. I could see on his face he knew the other reason I wouldn't be going home for break.

That I never wanted to go home again. Yeah, he'd definitely read between the lines.

Damn, why'd I have to be so forthcoming in my papers? But, just as *Gangster's Folly* had for Montrose, the assignments for his class had all seemed to pour out of me.

Maybe I should have edited a bit more, though.

"Well, if you want to get started with my project over the break, you're welcome to. I'll be different places over the break. I'm going to New York for a few days, to a wedding, then skiing."

"Yes, I'd like to start working on it. But, you know, you don't have to be around for it."

He nodded. "And self-sufficient. I knew you were the

right choice, Ms. O'Brien. Why don't you stop by my office tomorrow? I'll be there all day. I'll get you a key and show you the first boxes and get you started."

"Great," I said, unable to tamp down the smile of excitement that burst forth.

He seemed a little startled, almost took a step back. "I'm really excited about this. Like you said, a great big jigsaw puzzle." I hoped that took anything off my smile that might have unnerved him. *No sir, it has nothing to do with the fact that I'll get to work so closely with you for five whole months!*

He stepped aside and motioned for me to lead the way out the door, which I did.

I started to turn right, and he left, and we both stopped. "So, I'll see you tomorrow, then?" he asked.

"Yes. It'll probably be around eleven. I have one last final that should be done around then."

"I'll see you tomorrow." He started to turn away, then stopped and looked at me again with a question in his eyes.

"What?" I asked.

"Now that I'm no longer your instructor, do you mind if I drop the Ms. O'Brien thing?"

"No. God, no. Not at all."

He chuckled. Man, he looked so…edible when he smiled.

"Great. See you tomorrow, Syd." My name sounded good coming from that mouth.

"Okay…"

"Billy," he said, with a pointed look.

"Okay, Billy," I said.

Yeah, my name from his mouth was good. But saying his name, to him? Even better.

THREE

◈

I WALKED TO THE admin building after leaving Snyder Hall, where, apparently, I now had a second job.

Ten thousand dollars! It was probably the amount that would be stuffed in most of these Bribury students' stockings next week, but to me it was a fortune.

I started calculating how much it would take for me to get a place here for the summer and take some classes. Maybe Lily would want to stay and room together now that she and Lucas were completely solid. I hadn't been around them much, but she and Lucas seemed like they would not easily be separated for the summer.

He was an okay guy, and made Lily happy, but she could have done so much better.

Here we were in a sea of future movers and shakers—learning to become that ourselves—and she goes and falls in love with a townie janitor.

Whatever. If she was happy...

I just knew I was done with townies of any kind. Been there, done that. I wanted to belong to the world that these kids came from.

Maybe a little too desperately.

After the first week or so of classes, I had overheard two of the girls calling me a poser. Jane had come to my defense (none of them had seen me), which was kind of unusual because I think Jane had thought that about me herself.

We kind of came to a truce after that, Jane and I. On paper, we were nothing alike—she coming from a very prominent family (sort of), having been raised knowing that she'd be taken care of financially (with a few strings), and being an only child (well, she wasn't quite, but was raised as one).

But when you scratched the surface, Jane and I had a lot more in common than most would think.

We both had fractious relationships with our fathers (okay, at least she knew who her father was), we both felt out of place at Bribury (though she hid it better than I did), and we both could go toe-to-toe with anyone who wronged one of our own (though Jane would do it with her savage wit and I'd just call upon my Queens-born badass self).

Maybe Jane would want to stay here this summer too and the three of us could save money and find a cheap place off campus together. I knew Jane wanted to go home for the summer about as much as I did.

I checked in with my boss, Mrs. Otterbein, at the office of Administrative Affairs and got my schedule for the coming three weeks.

Score.

While my fellow students would be out binge drinking with their prep school posses, I would be clocking about thirty hours a week for the next three weeks.

I'd be able to buy gifts for the boys and send them home.

The feelings of guilt swamped me, as they did any time I thought of my younger half-siblings.

And, as I did all those other times, I pushed the feelings away, deep down, and thought about something pleasant.

Like ten thousand dollars buying me my freedom. At least for the summer.

When I got back to the dorm, Lily and Jane had already left for break. We'd known we would probably crisscross today and so we'd said our goodbyes last night, drinking from a bottle of champagne that Lily had supplied. (A perk of having an of-age boyfriend.)

We'd even done this silly thing that Lily had suggested—yeah, it wouldn't have come from Jane or me—where we each wrote down a sentence that started with "This time next year, I will…"

It was kind of hokey, but we couldn't say no to Lily. She'd said, "No bullshit like 'I'll be ten pounds lighter' or anything. Dig deep, ladies."

It felt kind of like a natural extension of the paper for Montrose's class that we'd each written. Who we were today, and I supposed, who we wanted to be in a year.

We'd made jokes about it, but the room had turned quiet as we'd all filled out our paper and sealed them up in individual envelopes, writing our names on the front.

Lily was the keeper of all three and said we'd open them next New Year's Eve, or as close as possible when we'd all be together.

We'd easily killed the bottle of champagne, then Lily and Jane had gone back to their room to start packing.

I'd seen postings on Instagram about the different parties around campus, and could have gone to one of them, but had stayed in.

Now, as I entered my room, even though I always had my own space, I could feel the emptiness of the suite.

I passed through the bathroom, Lily and Jane's stuff gone, the vanity looking a bit bereft and bare.

Their room was weird—the personal things on the walls and desktop were still there. Things like posters and framed photos. Their beds were made (which was not the norm for

Jane, but was for Lily). But there were gaping holes in their closets from clothes they'd taken home. And their desks had spaces where their laptops usually were, and where they charged all their stuff.

I checked the lock on their door, then went back to my room, leaving the door on the connecting bathroom unlocked.

I threw my coat on the back of my desk chair, then saw a small gift-wrapped package on my pillow.

Oh, great. We'd agreed not to exchange gifts. I wasn't sure if that was a pity move on Jane and Lily's part, so as to spare me the expense, or if they just didn't want to bother during finals.

I had adhered to our agreement, but it looked like Lily hadn't. Crap. I hated feeling like a charity case.

My issue, I knew, but…still. It was bad enough to feel it every time I pulled a shift at the admin building, as part of the work-study program.

But the present wasn't from Lily, it was from Jane. I unwrapped it slowly, knowing it would be the only Christmas gift I received.

My mother had clearly stated that there would be no money for a gift for me since I'd been selfish enough to leave and force her to find childcare for Duncan and Liam, which I'd done after school.

It was meant to make me feel guilty—and it had. But it also gave me a moment of delicious spite, knowing my mother would have to step up and take the place I'd been holding down for her for the past five years.

To hell with Christmas presents. It wasn't like she ever gave me much anyway.

Inside the small box was a silver medallion on a thin, beautiful silver chain. I held it up, letting it twist this way and that as the chain unraveled. It was some kind of symbol with rounded squares and ovals intertwined and a kind of loopy thing in the middle. It was different, and pretty, but not at all delicate.

I pulled out the card Jane had shoved at the bottom of the box. The handwriting was strong and bold—like Jane herself.

It's the Celtic symbol for strength. You've got it, babe, let people know it. Plus, your name is O'Brien, you should be rockin' some Celtic stuff.

Weird. Jane and I had started off rocky, but had come to get along well. Throughout the whole semester, we'd never had any really deep talks, though. Certainly none about our inner strength.

I put the necklace on and looked at myself in the mirror. I had carefully transformed myself to look like nearly every other girl on campus. Straightened long hair, worn either down like I had it now, or up in a sloppy bun. Subtle makeup, so it didn't look like I was trying. A North Face jacket, now hanging on the back of my chair. A hoodie, Lulus and Uggs.

A true Bribury Basic.

I took my hoodie off, throwing it on my bed, so I could see the pendant against my skin. I had on a low-vee, long-sleeved tee in fuchsia and the silver chain and pendant seemed to almost glow against my skin. Darker—*much*—than my mother's other children, I certainly didn't look like someone with the name O'Brien.

But, there were a lot of other ethnic-looking students here at Bribury. In fact, looks-wise, I stood out way more in my Irish Catholic neighborhood of Woodside, than I did here.

So, ethnic looking, yes…but which ethnicity? My mom would never answer any questions about my father, so I wasn't sure if I was half Hispanic, Italian, Middle-Eastern, or what.

I guessed it didn't matter, but it would have been cool to know my roots.

I ran a hand under the chain, lifting it off my skin so it

caught the light from my desk lamp. I didn't know what kind of message Jane was trying to send, but I did like the necklace. I hadn't seen any girls at Bribury wearing anything like it, and that kind of made me nervous to wear it.

But then I thought about Jane taking the time to pick this out because, for some reason, she wanted me to know she thought I was strong, and I decided it would be something I'd wear. Often. Maybe always.

I grabbed my phone out of my backpack, unpacking my other stuff too. The term paper from Montrose's class came out in my last handful and I placed it on the desk in front of me.

In a way, it was another present to open—to read all of his comments. Especially now that I knew he so diligently read these papers. He must, if he'd remembered so many details about me from previous papers.

I rubbed my hand along the front page, but before I indulged myself I texted Jane.

Thanks for the necklace. It's beautiful, and I love it.

Glad you liked it.

We said no gifts!

I know. I hadn't planned on it, but I saw this and thought of you.

I wanted to ask her why. What about the Celtic symbol of strength said "Syd" to her? Other than the Irish thing.

Instead, I just typed, *Thanks again. Are you home yet?*

Home. Hell. Whatever. Yeah, I'm here.

I smiled, thinking about Jane having to go home for Christmas and then standing in her half sister's wedding the week after.

And again I thought how lucky I was that Bribury was installing their new front end system over break, allowing me to not only make some extra money, but also have an excuse not to go home.

This is going to feel like the longest break ever, Jane texted.

I would be spending part of mine in Billy Montrose's office going through the notes of his next great novel.

To me, the break couldn't last long enough.

FOUR

·❖·

MY LAST FINAL WENT OKAY. Probably not four-point good, but good enough to keep my GPA in the range needed to keep my scholarship.

I made my way to Montrose's office in Snyder Hall.

He opened the door after I knocked, and stepped back, waving me in.

I took a couple of steps into his office and stopped.

"I know. It's bad, right?" he said, indicating the plethora of boxes lined and stacked…well, all over the place. Some were large, like the kind apples were shipped in. Some others were shoebox size.

"It's a lot, that's for sure," I said, trying not to sound daunted. I wanted this job, badly. And not just for the money and what it would mean to me.

It was likely as close as I would get to crawling inside the mind of a literary genius (okay, wunderkind, at least, if not genius) and I wanted that.

But, yeah, there were a *lot* of boxes, and this was going to take a lot of time.

"So, you decided to bring the boxes from your apartment over after all," I said.

He looked a little embarrassed as he said, "No. They're still there."

I nodded. "About the same amount as here?"

He looked around, taking stock. "Hmmm…maybe more. Probably more."

"Okay. Well, let me get a start on the boxes here while you're gone. I won't need keys to your apartment. Unless you think they should be worked on simultaneously, or something?"

He let out an exasperated sigh. "I have no idea how they should be worked on." He moved to his desk, the only uncluttered surface in the small room, and picked up a sheet of paper that he held out to me.

I walked the few feet to him and took the piece of paper. "What's this?"

"I put it together last night. It's a broad—like side of the barn, broad—breakdown of the characters' names and basic plot points of each of the different book ideas I have. Some even have working titles."

"Great," I said, scanning down the rather long list. He hadn't been kidding when he'd said he'd had a lot of different ideas for novels. "This will be really helpful." I meant it. Already my mind was thinking of ways to organize his notes, how the different puzzle pieces might fit together.

"I'm sure once you dig in, you'll find a lot of rogue notes. Some that don't belong to any of the book ideas on this." He tapped the back of the paper I still held, and it rippled in my hands. He sat on the edge of his desk. I wanted to look at his outline, but his guest chair had two boxes on it, so I leaned against the edge of his desk next to him.

We were close to each other, though not touching. His hand was on the desk, not far from my thigh.

He was wearing a black fleece pullover, with a hint of red tee showing at the neck. Blue jeans and pure white running shoes.

And he smelled like…sex. No, like intelligence. Like sexy

intelligence.

It was good he was going to be gone for three weeks—there was no way I'd be able to concentrate on his pile of boxes if he was here in this small room with me.

"Like Esme," he said, pointing to the name at the top of the paper I held. "I know before I decided on the name Esme, I called her something else in some of my notes, but I'm not really sure what."

"Esme. Got it." I looked around the room again. "Well, you've certainly got the *squalor* covered."

A laugh escaped him. It sounded like it almost hurt, like maybe he didn't do it very often. He chuckled along with us in class, but this was different.

"Yeah, the squalor for sure." He shook his head and gave an exaggerated puppy dog-eye look at me. "But not the *love.*"

I put my head down pretending to read his list. But I was really trying to hide the smile that came across my face because he got my Salinger reference, and for the playful look he gave me.

He'd always been somewhat jovial—if distracted—in class, but I would never say he'd been playful with us.

Guess I wasn't his student anymore in truth.

I looked back at him and he was staring down at me with humor and warmth. I couldn't hide my smile any longer, though I tried to damper it a bit from how happy this whole situation made me.

"Wow," he said, in almost a whisper. "You're a pretty girl, but when you smile…beautiful."

I started to look away, but didn't. This was not some Bribury boy to play flirty games with. Billy Montrose was a man, and if he wanted to tell me he liked my smile, I was going to look him in the eye as he did.

"Thanks," I said, trying to keep my voice light and breezy.

Like men I'd been obsessed with for five years told me I was beautiful all the time.

My frankness seemed to take him a little aback. He straightened, moving away from me just a tiny bit, as he studied me. "You didn't smile a lot in class," he said.

"Funny, when you laughed at my Esme joke, I was thinking you didn't do that in class…ever."

"I didn't?"

I shook my head. "Nope. Never an out-and-out laugh."

He turned his head straight ahead, looking toward the door. "Huh. I thought you guys cracked me up all the time."

"Well you, I don't know, chuckled with us. But never a big laugh like you just did."

Still looking at the door and not at me he said, "Was I a total dick? You can tell me. Your grades have already been submitted." There was a hint of joking in his voice, but I thought it sounded forced.

"No, not a dick at all. Just not a big wisecracker. Most profs aren't."

He shook his head, then looked back at me. "No I suppose not." Keeping his gaze steady on mine, he asked, "But was I pretentious as hell?"

I didn't look away, didn't hesitate as I said, "A little. But most profs are."

He laughed. Not the big laugh of earlier, but still a nice sound that let me know he appreciated my honesty. And that it was okay to bust his balls a little.

When his smile dimmed, he looked around the office, not really at just the numerous boxes, but seeming to take in the office itself. "Prof. I'm a prof—if not in credentials, certainly in duties."

"Yes," I said softly. It didn't really feel like he'd said it to me.

"Jesus, how did I get here?"

I stayed silent. It certainly wasn't my place to answer him.

He may not have liked the path which brought him to Bribury—the maze of boxes, and lack of a second novel, indicated that it'd been a frustrating route—but I was happy he was here.

He stepped away from the desk and immediately I missed the warm presence of his body next to mine. "Okay, Billy, enough self-pity for today," he said as he walked around the desk. "I've got three whole weeks with family that will trigger that particular emotion."

A small sound of part laughter and part commiseration escaped from me.

"You too?" he asked from behind me.

I turned to find him picking up his phone and scrolling through it. "Doesn't everybody?" I answered.

He looked up from his phone to me. "I suppose so, but it's the self-absorbed, pretentious fools like me that think it only applies to them."

He stared at me, almost challenging me.

"You're not…" I started. He raised his eyebrow at me. "A *fool.*"

For a split second his face didn't change, and I thought that maybe I'd blown the whole thing. That he'd say it wasn't going to work out. That I wouldn't be able to afford staying here for the summer and instead be forced to take care of the boys and not be able to take any kind of paying job.

But most devastating of all, I wouldn't get to work so closely to a man I greatly admired—pretentious and self-absorbed as he might be.

Then he burst out laughing and returned to his phone. "Oh, Syd, this is going to work out just fine."

As he clicked away, I relaxed, and mentally noted that he

liked when I told him what was what. Looking at the boxes around me, I wondered if that would apply to his work as well.

He held his phone out to me. "Here, put your number in so I have it, okay?"

"Of course." I took the phone from him, our fingers not touching at all. He'd already set up a contact page for me and all I did was add my number. I added my email too, although he would have had that on his class roster, but this saved him a step.

And really, wasn't that why I was earning a badly needed ten thousand dollars? To save Montrose a *major* step of sorting through five years of notes? Though by the number of boxes, it looked more like fifty year's worth.

I handed the phone back to him and he called me. I took my phone out of my back pocket and started to add the new number to my contacts.

"Syd," he said and I looked up. "Say cheese." He was holding the phone out, in a camera-holding way.

I automatically smiled. After all the social media my generation had been exposed to, when a phone was pointed at you…you posed.

"Is that okay?" he said after he took my picture. "I just like keeping photos on my contacts. I tend to forget names sometimes and this helps me."

"Sure," I said. Then held mine up and took a shot of him as he was looking down at his phone. He looked up, startled, when he heard the click. A corner of his mouth quirked up in a half-grin. He tipped his head a little in my direction, as if to say, "touché."

"Okay. I've got to get going or I'm going to miss my train." He looked as if maybe that wouldn't be such a bad thing. Then he let out a big sigh and said, "Yeah. I've got to go," as if trying to convince himself.

He came around to my side of the desk and handed me a key chain with a key card and two keys on it. "This one is for the building. And this one for my office. You have to use the key card if you enter the building when it's locked and you use the key. When you enter and leave. They need to know who's in the building in case of a fire or something."

I nodded, holding my hand open under his. He placed the keys on my palm. "The building is going to be open during regular office hours. I guess because of all the front end testing stuff?"

"Right," I said.

"But I'm guessing they'll be locked up on weekends and on actual Christmas and New Year's days, so…the key and key card."

"Got it." I wrapped my hand around the keys and put them in the front pocket of my jeans.

"Not that I'm saying you have to work weekends or anything. Again, you make your own schedule, I just want the job done before the end of next semester, so I can start digging in as soon as I'm done and back in New York."

"That's fine. But my next shift at the admin building isn't until Monday morning, so I had planned on getting started today and working this weekend."

"That's great. Oh, you mean, starting…today?"

I nodded. "Right after you leave."

He looked around at the boxes and it seemed like panic crossed his face. "Umm…yeah…well."

I grabbed his bulging satchel from the top of his desk and handed it to him. He numbly took it, looking at it like it was a foreign object.

"You're going to miss your train," I said. I grabbed his leather jacket from the coatrack in the corner by the door, and handed it to him. "You need to go." I pulled his arm, the warmth of him seeping through the fleece he wore.

"Right. Right," he said, moving to the door, but still looking around like he was leaving his newborn baby with a first-time sitter.

And perhaps that was exactly what he was doing.

I opened the door and gently pushed him out into the hallway. He was looking beyond me, back into his office, at his boxes. Then he focused on me, his eyes almost pleading.

I placed my hand on top of his, still clutching his jacket. "I'll take care of it," I said. He just stared at me, his face unreadable.

"I'll take care of *them*," I added, meaning his precious characters.

He took a deep breath and nodded, sensing I got how important the little people in the boxes were to him.

"Thank you," he whispered, then turned and walked down the hall.

I watched him walk away (who wouldn't enjoy that view!), waiting for him to turn around and come back to look at his babies once more.

But he didn't. He kept walking down the hall, turning at the stairwell.

I returned to his office, shut and locked the door, pulled off my North Face, and set about organizing Billy Montrose's next great novel.

FIVE

MY PHONE DINGED with a text, pulling me out of my Montrose's notes-induced haze. I was sitting on the floor of his office, one box's contents forming a circle around my crossed legs. Reaching for my phone, which was in the pocket of my jacket, I tried not to mess up my various piles.

You still there? A text from Montrose.

I looked at the time—nine at night. God, I'd been here working for almost nine hours. I vaguely remembered going down the hall to the ladies' room once, and pulling a Diet Coke from my backpack, but other than that, I hadn't moved much from my spot on the floor.

Yes, I texted back.

Have you gone back to your room and come back, or have you been there the entire time?

The entire time.

Jesus. You've got five months, you know.

I thought I'd just get a start on organizing the different boxes. Putting the boxes in order by the dates on your notes.

And? That should have taken you a few hours, tops. He texted when I didn't type anything further.

And…I got sucked in.

Tell me about it, he responded.

My thumbs were poised over my phone, but I wasn't sure

what to say next. Did I tell him how much I enjoyed this job, even though it was only my first day? (Would that sound like sucking up?) Did I relay how much more solidified my idea of him as a great author was, by just reading notes he'd scribbled? (That would definitely sound like sucking up.)

Before I could decide what to text, my phone rang with a call from Montrose.

"Hi," I said, then put the phone on speaker and rested it on my thigh as I carefully unbent my legs and stretched them out, bending forward to touch my toes.

"Hi," he said, his voice low and throaty. It instantly conjured up how good he'd smelled when he sat next to me on the ledge of his desk earlier. Seemed like I could almost still smell his spicy scent. "I forgot to tell you, there are a bunch of delivery menus and an envelope with some cash for you in the middle top drawer of my desk."

"Cash?" I asked. My first payment for this job was to come January first, ten days away, and I hadn't expected cash—though that would be great.

"For food for when you're working there and want something to eat."

"You didn't have to do that. I can bring or buy my own food," I said with a bit of defensiveness in my voice. A prickle of what Jane called my Chip (it was a proper noun to her) rose to the back of my neck.

"I know you can. But with the hours you'll be working for admin, and then in my office, my guess is you won't get to the caf a lot during their limited hours over break."

He was right, and I'd thought about that. All the cafs but one were closed for break, and the one that would feed the students here over the holidays had limited hours. I figured I'd be making a lot of pit stops at the convenience store just off campus. And of course, delivery. But I tried to keep both those options at a minimum because of my tight budget, preferring to get most of my meals at the caf, which was included in my scholarship program.

"Well…I…"

"Listen, it's not charity. I know this is your second job, and you'll be doing it at odd hours. And I know from experience how easy it is to let time get away from you when immersed in a project. This was just an employer making allowances for his employee's diligence."

"Wow, that sounds so…corporate."

He laughed. "Hardly. My guess is you're camped out on the floor with my crap piled all around you. Not real executive of a setting."

"Do you have a camera in here?" I said, kind of teasing, but dang his description was spot on.

"Like a nanny cam?" He chuckled, and I envisioned the corner of his mouth lifting slightly as it had when I'd seen him earlier today. "What would we even call that? A literary assistant cam?"

"Is that what I am? A literary assistant?"

I could almost see him shrug. Strange that I'd so quickly become attuned to his body language after so short of a time. Though, I had been watching him—closely—three times a week for the past four months.

"I thought it had a more prestigious ring than box unpacker. It might look good on a résumé, depending on what types of jobs you'll be looking for in three and a half years."

"God, I *so* don't want to think about that yet."

He didn't say anything for a moment, and when he did respond, it was with a quiet, low voice. "But you *do* think about it, don't you, Syd? You think about your future all the time. Just so you don't have to think about where you come from."

I slowly eased my body out of my stretch, the phone

moving slightly on my thigh. Reaching out to hold it in place, I felt another prickle on my neck. Not Chip this time, but something much deeper. Much darker.

"Yes," I answered, not wanting to admit the truth.

"Sorry," he said. "Didn't mean to get all heavy on you."

"That's okay," I replied, even though his insight was a bit unnerving.

There was a pause, and then he switched tone and topic with, "Have you ever thought about being a writer? Your stuff is so…honest. I know they were just papers for a freshman class, but, still."

I'd never in my life thought about becoming a writer, even though I loved to read. But when he said that…yeah, the prickles again. Prickle city.

It felt like that kids' game, where you put the squares and circles in the right hole. And I'd been trying to get the green triangle in the red square hole. And then, when he said "be a writer" I suddenly saw the triangle opening just a few inches away.

My imaginary hand hovered over the correct hole, and then I pulled it back, setting it down.

"Are you kidding?" I said to Montrose. "No way."

"Why not? It's a noble profession."

"Yeah, if you're the National Book Award winner," I said.

He, of course, *was* the National Book Award winner five years ago for *Folly*.

And hadn't published since.

"Oh, come on, that's not fair," he said. He was right, it wasn't.

A thought occurred to me. "Wait. This job. My papers. This isn't some kind of whole Pygmalion thing, is it?"

"Christ, I'm only twenty-eight. I'm still learning myself. Do you really think I'm Henry Higgins material?"

I had a flash of that *Seinfeld* episode where Elaine mispronounces Svengali, just as he added, "Or a Svengali." He mispronounced it just like Elaine had in the episode, with a soft G.

"Okay, Elaine," I said, and he laughed—loudly and naturally.

"I figured you'd be too young to get that one," he said.

"We're both too young to get it," I answered.

But apparently we'd both been big *Seinfeld* rerun bingers. We spent the next half hour comparing notes on our fave episodes and lines *("No, I mentioned the bissssque"* was a shared one).

I laid back on the floor, reaching my arms over my head for a better stretch, and setting my phone in the crook of my shoulder.

He did a great Bania impression that had tears of laughter rolling down the sides of my face.

"You're funny," I said, catching my breath.

"You seem surprised by that," he said.

I thought about that. "I guess I am. I mean, you can be light in class, but, like, no impressions or anything."

"Damn, and I was going to incorporate my Tolstoy impression into next semester."

I laughed again, then said, "But *Gangster's Folly* was so…"

"Not funny?"

I thought about the book. I had read it ten times easily, though no other time had been so important, so monumental, as the first.

"Well, I mean, there were funny *parts* in it. Like the scene where he's trying to get Stef into bed—"

"Based on actual events, I might add."

I smiled to myself, but continued, "But on the whole, it's so dark. A tragedy, really."

"That's your take? A tragedy?"

I shrugged and my phone slipped from my shoulder. I caught it and readjusted.

"What was that?" he asked.

"Phone slid off me. All's well now."

"Slid *off* you? How was it *on* you?"

"I'm lying on the floor. It was on my shoulder."

There was nothing from him and I checked my phone to make sure I hadn't disconnected. Nope.

"So, back to *Folly*?" I said finally, after the silence. I figured he was doing something else, and now that we'd finished up the *Seinfeld* conversation, he was bored and wanted to end the conversation. Appealing to his inner preening artist, I tried to pull it back to him…or at least his book.

"Um, maybe I shouldn't say this…" he said.

"What?" I asked. Was he going to tell me some secret about *Folly* that no one else knew? Like what Aidan whispered to Stef that made her say yes?

"All thoughts of *Folly* rushed out of my head—perhaps forever—when you mentioned that you're lying on the floor of my office."

"Why? Is that bad? Did someone die on this floor or something? I mean, I know it's not crazy clean, but believe me, I've—"

"Is your hair down? Loose?"

"Why? Is there something on the carpet?"

He chuckled, but this was a different sound. Deep and throaty, and it almost caught in his throat.

Ohhhhh.

"Yes, my hair is loose," I said. Not in any kind of temptress voice (not that I even had one in my toolkit), but not in a no-nonsense tone either. Just a calm, low voice.

Another long silence, which this time I had no intention

of breaking with questions about his book.

After a few seconds I heard him take a deep breath and slowly let it out. "You know, I think I'm just a little weirded out today. Coming back to the city, staying with my parents. My apartment being sublet. This whole year is kind of weirding me out."

I didn't say anything, this was his ramble. I didn't want to tip the scales one way or another, though I wasn't even sure what was being weighed.

Well, I sort of did. I'd known about *those* kind of scales for way too long.

"I...I just don't want to seem creepy or anything," he finally said.

"You didn't. You don't."

Another long exhale. "Good. Good. Listen, I'm supposed to meet friends downtown for drinks. I better get going."

"Okay," I said, then waited for him to say goodbye. Which he didn't.

"It's just that...I mean..." More silence. "Yeah, I'm gonna go."

"Okay," I said again.

"Syd?"

"Yes?"

"Thanks for taking the job," he softly said.

"Thanks for offering it."

"Good night."

"Good night."

He was gone. And I laid on the floor of his office for a long time before I finally got up, pulled forward the notes I wanted to work on tomorrow, then went home to my dorm room.

And thought the whole time about what he'd said—and more importantly, what he *hadn't* said.

SIX

***

"**WHAT BOX ARE YOU** working on now?" he asked when he called me the next day. It was around one in the afternoon and I'd been there since nine working.

"Rachel," I said.

"No, Billy," he teased.

"Ha. Ha. I'm working on the box with all the Rachel notes."

"Rachel? I don't have a Rachel."

"I'm thinking she's what Esme either started as or morphed into, or—"

"Oh, Rachel, that's it. Yeah, I know her," he said, like he'd just remembered the name of someone he ran into somewhere but hadn't seen for a while. In a way, that's exactly what it was. Going through his notes made me realize that these people, these characters, were real to him. Friends.

There would be innocuous items, like body type, race, coloring, that sort of thing, so he could keep the visual straight once he was writing. But then there would be this random note like "When she was in second grade, she wanted fashion-y boots, but her mother made her wear her current, dorky snow boots because they were still in good shape. So she took a butter knife (the only kind she was allowed to handle—she might have been a bit of a rebel, but some rules she knew better than to break) and pierced her boots so her mother would have to buy her new ones." And wrapped around that piece of paper was a cocktail napkin from some place I'd heard of in Manhattan with "don't use this...just for character development" scribbled on it with red Sharpie.

"So, I'm creating a 'possibly Esme' pile. That's what I'm working on."

"You can scratch the 'possibly' part. She was Rachel for a few months in there for sure."

I looked at the box, nearly full except for the pieces I had piled in front—and to the side, and to the back—of me on the same spot on the floor I'd sat yesterday.

These were all notes he'd done on *one* character in a few months? Good lord, the man must have done nothing for the past five years but write plot and character notes.

And yet, no novel to show for all of the labor that sat around the room, surrounding me.

"So, you're going with Esme? Rachel and Esme, same person?"

"Yes," he said.

I hesitated too long, and he was starting to know me. "What?" he asked.

"Nothing," I quickly said. What I was thinking was not my place to say.

"What?" he said with exasperation in his voice.

"Well, it's not really important."

"Is it about my stuff? My work?"

"Uh...yeah."

"Then spill."

"No, really—"

"Come on, Syd. I hired you, I want any feedback you want to give."

"I would never presume to give you...feedback." Even the

idea seemed preposterous to me.

"At least I've read your stuff, your papers—and liked them. Most of the feedback I get is from hack critics who couldn't write a grocery list and so they have to bring others down."

Huh. That sounded out of character for the person I'd gotten to know—albeit only in the last couple of days, three months of one-sided lectures, and one *Seinfeld*-bonding phone call.

He snorted, and added, "Or at least that's what my agent and editor say to me."

Yeah, that sounded about right. "And what do you say?"

Another snort. "Nothing. I just let them blow smoke up my ass until I am properly soothed."

"Well let's face it, there wasn't a lot of negative feedback on *Gangster's Folly* anyway, was there?" I mean, it had won a bunch of awards and still lingered at the bottom of several best-seller lists five years later.

"Oh, there were a few. But yeah, it was well received. My ruffled feathers were more recent as it seems more and more people in the New York literary scene are getting in some shots about the wait on my next book."

He traveled in New York literary circles.

A vision of Dorothy Parker and her gang at the Algonquin popped into my head and I saw Montrose sitting amongst them in a smoke-filled room, throwing out bon mots and looking debonair. His tousled, tired, world-weary look fitting right in.

It was hard to imagine that he and I lived in the same country let alone the same city.

"But enough of that, I don't want to get pissed, it's the holidays." He let out a little laugh. "Though the holidays seem to bring out the pissed-off-edness in a lot of people."

A vision of my stepfather drunkenly knocking over our pathetic excuse for a Christmas tree flashed in my mind, but before I could agree with Montrose's summation, he added, "Seriously. What thought did you have about the Esme/Rachel thing?"

"Well, it seems like *Folly* was compared a lot to Salinger, particularly *Catcher in the Rye*."

"Yes?"

"How did you feel about that?" I'd wondered about that for a few years, but of course I didn't mention that part.

A long sigh. I started to lie back, but stayed in my position, not wanting to take any chances that he'd ask if I was lying down and then feel weird and want to end the call.

Because I could talk books all day with Billy Montrose. And it seemed I was getting my chance.

"At first I was incredibly flattered. I mean, I *love* Salinger, you know?" I nodded, but of course he couldn't see me. He went on like he could. "And then it got kind of annoying. This was *my* book. *My* work. *My* ideas. I got a chip on my shoulder about it. Those were what I endearingly call my 'prick years.'"

"When was this?" I asked.

"The last two years."

"You don't seem too much like a prick now. Are you out of that phase?"

"Depends on the day. That's why I'm here. Well, not *here*, at my parents', but at Bribury. I didn't like what I was becoming."

"A prick?"

"Oh, I had fully become a prick. The next stage I seemed to be careening toward was 'self-entitled prick', and it was coming hard and fast."

"So, Bribury."

"Yeah. I used the excuse that I needed a change of scenery to 'get out of my head,' in order to write the next book. And that's true, but I knew I was just one martini-soaked, three-hour lunch away from being someone I didn't want to be. Because I had the sneaking suspicion that *he* couldn't write for shit."

I laughed at that. And kind of marveled at his self-awareness. Given the chance, I'd probably be perfectly happy to become a self-entitled prick and enjoy all the perks that came with it.

"Anyway. You don't want to hear all that." Oh, I so did! "Why the Salinger question?"

"Well, if there were all the Salinger comparisons, why would you bait that by having your protagonist named Esme? Seems like you're waving a red cape at them."

An out-and-out chuckle from him now. "Is it possible that we really just 'met' yesterday? Are you sure you haven't been organizing the files of my shrink?"

Ooh, he had a shrink—so Manhattan. There was a couch I'd like to lie on with him. And not in *that* way. Okay, in that way, too, but I'd love to hear the deep thoughts he spilled to his therapist.

"Yeah, that's where Rachel came in. At first, always, she was Esme in my head. But…my own Esme if that makes sense."

"It does."

"And I loved her. I wanted to write her, to be her. I could easily spend a whole book with her. And then I realized I was playing into their hands and I'd be crucified if I used the name Esme."

"So she became Rachel."

"Right."

"I'm not through everything here—*obviously*—but I think the dates on your notes show that you went back to Esme. Is that right?"

"Yeah, that was when the prick started rearing his head." (I can't even mention what visual *that* turn of phrase conjured up for me.) "And I was all 'Fuck you, he doesn't own the name.

I can do great things with my Esme too.'"

"Wow."

He let out a sigh, but I could see—hear—the smile on his face. "I know, right? Total prick."

"Well…hubris at the very least."

"Right. Exactly. Esme hubris."

"The very worst kind."

"Yes. But I couldn't see it at the time."

"Because you'd become a prick." There was no question in my voice.

"Yes, as we've established. So that's where we left off. With Esme."

"The 'fuck you Esme.'"

"Yes." He let out a big breath, like he'd just told me a piece of gossip that he'd been dying to repeat. And maybe that was exactly what he'd done.

"Okay. One pile for all Esme or Rachel related notes. Future name to be determined," I said.

I smiled as he laughed on the other end, then said goodbye.

SEVEN

"SHE'S AN ESME," I said when I picked up his call.

"I know, right?"

"But…"

"Yeah? A 'but?' It's okay, give it to me."

I was back in his office, having gotten there early, wanting to get back to work. Had I ever wanted to get to work?

Plus, I needed to leave in time to take the bus to the mall before it closed.

Knowing I'd probably be too engrossed in Montrose's notes to notice the time later, I had set the alarm on my phone to go off in time for me to leave.

I'd been there about four hours when Montrose called.

"She's Salinger's Esme," I broke the news to him.

"Fuck."

"Maybe I shouldn't have said—"

"No, no. I'm glad you did. Are you sure? I mean there's not much even written yet, no prose or anything, bits of dialogue and character notes."

"Well, then, maybe…" But there was doubt in my voice and he knew it.

"Fuck," he said again. "I believe you. And, shit, I think I knew it."

"It's just…it's her. Practical. Unsentimental. Wise beyond

her years. Very matter-of-fact. And yet you know she's going to rip your heart out. I'm sorry," I said. It almost felt like consoling someone whose friend had just died. "I think," I started, wanting to throw him a bone, "it's because of these notes about her as a kid. They just feel so…so…Esme, you know?"

"Yeah," he said, dejection—almost resignation—in his voice.

"But maybe if you just left those out? I mean, some of them even say 'do not use, just for character development,' so maybe if they're not actually in the book?"

"Yeah, maybe," he said, his voice perking up a little bit.

"I mean, obviously *I'm* looking for it since you pointed it out, and I'm reading all these notes about her as a child, probably right around Salinger's Esme's age…"

"Yeah, that's true." More hope in his voice now.

"I don't think you need to scrap her totally."

"No?" he asked, like I was his editor or something, not just some college freshman who had no point of reference on what made a novel a masterpiece—other than having read many of them.

"But, you should probably go with Rachel, not Esme."

A long, loud sigh on the other end. "Yeah, I guess."

He asked me about the notes I'd gone through today and I answered him. I'd taken a stack and brought them to his desk, not wanting to spend another day on the floor. So I sat in his chair, going through his stuff and inputting it into some of the different spreadsheets and Word docs I'd already begun, while he spoke on the phone to me.

It was definitely surreal.

I was listening to him, but my eyes wandered to the framed photos on his desk. One of him and his parents taken at his graduation from Brown.

He looked like his mother—very Upper East Side, very

Old Money. She was in a smart, cream linen suit. My guess was Chanel, but I'm not well versed on WASP-wear. Montrose had his arm around her, a near-identical smile on both their faces.

His father was on his other side and also wore what looked like a cream linen suit, though definitely not Chanel. Brooks Brothers maybe? His arm was not slung around his son or his wife's shoulder, but there was a nice smile on his face and he seemed happy to be in the photo.

The other photo was of Montrose and a beautiful young woman, their arms entwined, both looking at the camera. They wore ski gear and I could see a ski resort, and mountain, behind them.

"Uh-huh," I said to Montrose, not catching everything he said, but most of it. I slid my laptop over and Googled "Billy Montrose girlfriend" and waited. Several times the name Diandra Scott came up, but upon further investigation, it looked like they'd ended things a while ago. And on Google images Diandra Scott was not the woman skiing with him. A new girlfriend? He looked about his current age in the photo, like maybe it had been taken last winter.

"Um," I said, when he paused, "I'm working at your desk today, and I was just noticing the photos on your desk."

"I have photos on my desk? I don't think so."

"Yeah, I'm looking right at them."

"Seriously? Like, framed photos of people?"

Man, absent-minded professor or what? "Yes. Two of them. And you're in both photos."

"I don't think—Oh. Oh, right. My mom sent those to me when I first started at Bribury. She sent them right to the office. Probably figured—rightfully so—that I wouldn't take the time to put up anything personal. I just sat them on the desk and didn't think of them again."

"But you must see them every day."

"Yeah, I guess."

I was desperate to ask about his ski bunny when he said, "One with them at Brown, right? And one of me and my sister skiing?"

An easing in my heart at hearing the word "sister," and then self-chastisement. Like it should even matter to me if he had a girlfriend or not.

But it did. It desperately did.

"Right, those are the two," I said.

"Yeah, of course I remember. Like you said, I see them every day."

I laughed as I ran my finger along the heavy, expensive silver frame. "Oh yeah? What is your mother wearing in this photo?"

"A Chanel suit."

"Huh. I guess you do notice them."

He didn't say anything for too long. "Wait," I said. "She always wears Chanel suits, doesn't she?"

"Busted."

We laughed together, and it felt so good, so right, to share something with him.

After talking about Esme/Rachel for another hour we said our goodbyes and hung up. I wanted to dive back into his notes, but the Google page with results on Montrose taunted me until I finally mentally packed my bags and spent the next two hours cyber stalking him.

There wasn't much I didn't already know, although I hadn't been aware of his relationship with Diandra Scott—a woman he apparently met at Brown and dated quite seriously for several years. If I did my math correctly, I estimated they'd broken up right about the time he felt he was heading for self-entitled prick. So, he'd been a prick for about two years of their relationship. Maybe Diandra dumping him is what made him take a hard look at his life?

Or maybe he'd dumped her because of said prick-ness?

At one time, I'd known everything there was to know about Billy Montrose. In fact, I probably should have guessed that the woman in the second photo was his twin sister. They had a very similar look, though the sister was blond to Montrose's dark brown hair. But the same eyes, the same perfect smile with blindingly-white teeth.

But I was kind of shocked that I'd never Googled for his girlfriend before.

Well, no, not totally shocked.

It would never have been in my realm of thought that I should. To me, he was the author of the book that changed my life. I hadn't thought of him in terms of even having a personal life. I'd only wanted to read about him as it related to *Gangster's Folly*.

Until now.

Until I'd sat in front of him three days a week and felt this deep connection that no doubt every other female in his classroom did.

Until I lay on the floor of his office and knew he liked that image, that it made him uncomfortable.

I hadn't come to Bribury because Montrose was to be a guest instructor for a year. I hadn't even known that when I'd applied. But by the time I got the offer of a scholarship to Bribury and a few other schools (one of them a legit Ivy League school, not just a wannabe), I'd found out that Montrose would be at Bribury.

I took it as a sign, and sent in my acceptance of their offer that same day.

My alarm went off, interrupting my Google frenzy and I was glad that I wasn't being paid by the hour or I would have felt terribly guilty, or not counted the past two hours or something.

Funny, I never felt that guilt in my admin job. There, I was happy to have nothing to do and get some studying in on their time.

I packed up and, with reluctance, left his office.

Taking the bus to the Schoolport mall, I thought about where I would start back in tomorrow, even though I'd have to put in my eight-hour shift at the admin building first.

I went to the shoe department of Macy's looking for the combat boots I'd travelled across town for, cursing the fact that I'd have to spend some of my precious discretionary funds on something I didn't even particularly like.

I mean, I'd been to this mall too many times over the semester, spending too much of my precious money, making sure I had what would make me blend in with the other Bribury girls. It seemed like Lily had known exactly what to bring—I don't think she had gone shopping even once since we'd arrived.

And Jane couldn't be bothered with things like trends and fashions. I swear she got most of her clothes at thrift stores and Navy surplus places. She always looked cool and funky, but Jane was the type of personality that could carry that off. I wasn't.

It was a struggle for me, never having been one that cared that much about clothes, mainly because we couldn't afford latest trends when the boys' feet were growing so fast.

But I didn't want any of the girls at Bribury to know that, and so I came to school with what I thought was a good start, but every time a trend shifted—even slightly—I was back at the mall.

I had purchased a few pairs of Lulus in September, and had worn them with running shoes at first, then Uggs when it got colder, and depending on what I was wearing on top. But just before break I saw three different girls wearing them with combat boots and knew I'd be spending the money I'd set aside for Christmas gifts for the boys on new boots for myself.

Which made me feel like shit, but wouldn't keep me away from the mall.

But now, with Montrose's money coming in, I could afford both.

I stood in front of the rack and two different styles—two different brand names—of the boots commanded my attention.

Oh, God. I hadn't taken a close enough look at which type those girls were wearing. What if I got the wrong brand?

I'd just told a National Book Award winner that he had to change his protagonist's name without batting an eye. But now, thinking I might get the wrong kind of boot? Absolutely terrified.

"Most of the Bribury girls we see in here are going for this kind," a sales lady said to me, handing over the—naturally— more expensive brand.

"Are you sure?" I asked. It probably sounded to her like I was hoping it was the cheaper kind, and I was, but more importantly, I really just wanted to make sure I got the right kind.

I knew it was stupid, and I ultimately didn't even *like* the Bribury Basic look, but I just…couldn't stand out as the Queens white trash that I was.

That I had been. Because I'd vowed to leave *that* Sydney O'Brien back in Queens.

The sales lady murmured her confirmation and I bought the boots.

I went to Old Navy and got some cheap shirts and jeans for the boys. I found some perfume on sale, which I purchased for my mother. Picking up some wrapping paper, I figured I could run to the Post Office on my lunch hour tomorrow and get it all shipped to arrive by Christmas Eve on Wednesday. Shipping would probably cost me as much as the gifts themselves at this last moment, but that's what I got for putting it off.

On the bus ride home, I thought about the combat boots and battled with feelings of self-loathing for yet again caving to the feeling of wanting to fit in, and also a feeling of jubilation that, come January, I *would* fit in with those girls.

Lying in bed later that night, trying to sleep and wishing I could hear the sounds that Jane and Lily usually made in the other side of the suite, I wondered if Diandra Scott, or Billy Montrose's sister, had ever felt such fear as I had standing in front of a rack of boots?

No, probably not.

EIGHT

❖

Monday and Tuesday there were only brief texts from Montrose and I thought that maybe I'd lost him.

Not that I'd ever "had" him, in whatever context that meant. But maybe he'd had some second thought about just how involved he wanted me to be after the whole Rachel/Esme thing Sunday.

I worked during the day at the admin building, and at other places around campus, helping with the testing of the new system.

Not that I was a techie or anything—far from it. But we students weren't really testing that part, we were just entering mock data, like grades and stuff, in a "sandbox" environment (that's what the tech guys called it when they'd trained us) at various points across campus to see if the new system worked.

We were doing that all week. Then the tech team would look for errors, work them out, and then they'd do a conversion of all real data to the new system in the "live" environment, and then we'd spend the next week testing that.

I think some of the students who stayed to work (most of them were international students who didn't want to make the treks home) were hoping they'd be able to break the new system or something. There was an awful lot of consultants and technical people (student workers included) who were big time into this project.

I was just happy for the full workweeks for the next three weeks and what it would do for my bank account.

Well, almost full workweeks. We had Wednesday afternoon off for Christmas Eve, and Christmas day off. And the same schedule the following week, too, for New Year's.

So, I didn't even get to Montrose's office until after five both Monday and Tuesday.

I told myself that was the reason he just briefly texted to see if I had any questions each night.

I thought about making up a bogus question just so he'd call and I could hear his voice. It was amazing how much I missed hearing him after only a few days. Well, I had grown accustomed to his lecturing to me several times a week. Except, I didn't seem to miss my other profs.

But, I didn't give him a reason to call. If I'd pissed him off about the Salinger's Esme thing, then he had every right not to want my opinion on anything else. Resolving myself to just do the job asked of me, and not offer any extra curricular thoughts, I plowed through three more boxes during the two evenings I was there.

As it turned out, I was doing testing from Snyder Hall on Wednesday, so when my shift was over, I only had to walk down to the first floor to Montrose's office. Two more boxes were tackled, and I now had six very distinct piles going along the top of the credenza, which spanned one entire wall of his office. And only three more boxes to get to.

I was looking through the piles, debating whether to start transcribing each pile here in the office, or wait until I'd gone through the boxes in his apartment and do all the transcribing at once, when my phone dinged with Montrose's text tone. (Yes, I'd given him his own tone. Like, the second after he texted me the first time.)

You at home?

Not yet. Still in the office.

My office?

It wasn't like I had an office of my own. *Yes, your office. Will be going home in another hour or so.* I wanted to catch the caf before it closed. They were doing an earlier dinner for Christmas Eve, then not open at all tomorrow.

Taking the bus? Or train? He asked.

To my dorm? Neither. Just walking. I wasn't getting what he was asking.

By "home" I meant New York.

Oh. *I meant my dorm room.*

Not going home until tomorrow morning?

Not at all. I told you I was staying here over break. That's why I was able to get so much done so far.

Well, yeah, but I figured you'd go home for Christmas at least. And maybe New Year's.

Nope.

There was nothing from him for a full minute and I was both hoping and dreading that he'd forego the texting and call me. I desperately wanted to hear his throaty voice, but I couldn't bear to hear any pity in it because I would be alone on the holiday.

But you could go home if you wanted, right? I mean, you're not just staying because of my work?

My thumbs hovered above the keyboard on my phone. I could give lots of excuses for not being able to go home without him feeling responsible. And the truth was I wasn't staying because of his job, although that was making this whole break so much more enjoyable.

But I didn't want to lie to Montrose.

Yes. I could go home. If I wanted to.

Another long pause. I braced for a barrage of questions, or even for the phone to ring. But neither happened. Just a simple *Got it.*

He'd read my papers, some of them talking about my home life. None of them mentioned the *real* reason I never wanted to go home again, even though I missed my little brothers Duncan and Liam terribly.

So, yeah, even though he didn't know the whole story, and stories like mine didn't happen much in the Upper East Side, I think he did "get it."

I slept in on Christmas, and it felt wonderful. Until I thought of my brothers opening my presents to them and not being there to see their faces. It was just clothes, anyway, nothing that would make them beam with glee like a new toy would. But I knew they'd need clothes more than ever without me there to hound my mother and stepfather that they needed them.

I rolled over in bed, shutting out thoughts of the scene in Queens, and for a half second considered staying in bed all day, something I'd never had the luxury to do, even when I was sick.

Then I thought about the lovely piles of characters I was fast becoming friends with, just waiting for me in Montrose's office, and I flung my covers off and headed for the shower.

As I knew they would, the characters, and his notes, sucked me in, and it was four in the afternoon before I came out of my daze. And only because Lily called to wish me a Merry Christmas.

We talked for a half hour, her mostly filling me in on how her parents were taking her bringing Lucas home with her to meet them. (Apparently okay.)

She asked me how the admin testing job was going and I told her a little about it. I would have much more enjoyed talking about the job I was doing for Montrose, but for some reason, I didn't even mention to Lily that I'd picked up a second job.

After we hung up, I wondered about that—why I didn't talk about it with Lily. It wasn't like Montrose asked me to keep it a secret or anything. And though I had no intention of mentioning any specifics about his notes (not that Lily or Jane would care, but plenty of folks in the New York literature world probably would) there was no harm in saying I was doing filing for him.

And despite my wish for it to be more, based on the two great conversations I'd had with Montrose about his work, I basically *was* just helping him with his filing.

Certainly, if it had ever been more, it was back to note straightening and transcribing now.

Jane called next, and I wondered if Lily texted her and told her to call me. But, if Jane was making a pity call, she hid it well, spending the duration of the call bitching about her mother driving her nuts and the upcoming wedding of her half sister, of which Jane was a reluctant bridesmaid.

That was the thing with Jane—it very well *could* have been a pity call, which she covered by talking only about herself. Or, it could have just been Jane bitching, as she did semi-frequently.

Either way, it was good to hear their voices.

I hadn't even gotten back to work after Jane's call when my phone rang again with a number I didn't recognize. It was a local area code.

"Hello?" I answered.

"Sydney O'Brien?" a man with a very heavy Chinese accent asked.

"Yes?" I said hesitantly. Not really comfortable with confirming my name as I sat alone in a deserted building on an empty campus. But, he did know my name, and he had my number…

"I have delivery for you. Out front of Snyder Hall. Please come to door."

"What kind of delivery?" I flipped through stuff on Montrose's desk, looking for a campus phone directory to have security's number if needed.

"Dinner. Dinner from Peking Delight for Sydney O'Brien. That you?"

"Yes, it's me. But I didn't order anything, so—"

"Order from a Mr. Montrose. All paid for. Said to deliver to you here. You no want?"

I had grabbed my keys and keycard and was through the door as I was answering, "I want. I'll be right there."

He'd paid for dinner, even the tip. And it was an enormous amount of food, with appetizers, a couple of entrees and almond cookies. He'd even included a couple of Diet Cokes. It was all very thoughtful.

He was no self-entitled prick any longer, if he'd ever even been close.

I cleared off his desk and laid out my wonderful Christmas dinner. Most people would lament not having a home-cooked dinner on the holiday. But I knew my mother's cooking, and I was much happier with Peking Delight's offerings, non-traditional as they were.

About half an eggroll into my feast, my phone buzzed with a call from Montrose. Not just a call, but a FaceTime call. I contemplated how I looked for about a half second, until I realized it was more important to get the call before he hung up than run my fingers through my hair and put on lip gloss. Instead of answering on my phone, I slid my laptop over in front of me, careful to not drag it through crab rangoons and duck sauce, and took the call.

I wanted to see Montrose on a screen larger than my

phone.

"Merry Christmas," he said when his face appeared on my screen. It seemed like he was on a laptop too, given how much of the room behind him I was seeing. He looked like his normal self, and yet…so…damn sexy. Deep brown hair tousled and looking like he'd just gotten out of bed. Tired face with a few days of beard growth, but with those intense, intelligent grey eyes looking straight at me. Or at least at the image of me. He had his laptop tilted at an angle so I just saw his head and the upper part of the room behind him. Lovely, tasteful drapes and an ornate tray ceiling.

"Merry Christmas to you, too. Thank you for the dinner. You ordered way too much. But it's fabulous."

"You're welcome. And I was thinking you could put the leftovers in the fridge in the corner for some other meal. There's a microwave in the closet that you could pull out—I've never used it, I seldom have any leftovers when I order from there. Peking Delight has indeed been a delightful find in Schoolport."

"We haven't discovered them yet, but I'll for sure be letting Jane and Lily know about them when they get back."

"That would be Ms. Winters and Ms. Spaulding?"

"Yes," I said, growing just a tiny tense speaking of Jane in front of him. I tried not to let it show on my face, by taking a sip of my soda.

"I knew you all sat together in class. I didn't realize you were roommates."

"Technically Lily and Jane are roommates, and they're both my suitemates."

He nodded and I waited, my breath still, to see if he'd ask more about Jane.

"Did I catch you right in the middle of eating?"

The angle of my laptop caught my full plate, so I just shrugged and said, "That's okay. It will keep."

"No, go ahead and eat while it's still hot. I really just…"

"What?" I coaxed.

"Nothing. I should get going too."

"Have you already done Christmas dinner?" I asked, then took a bite of my eggroll, as if to prove to him he wasn't keeping me from my meal.

"Yeah, we got done about an hour ago. My parents went to friends of theirs for after dinner drinks. My sister and her boyfriend went to his parents' place."

I took another bite of eggroll and made a "mmm, goood" face while I chewed. "Not that anything would taste better right now—thanks, again—but what did your mom make for dinner?"

He laughed, and much as I loved hearing him laugh on the phone, it was so much better to be able to see him. To watch how his grin turned to a smile. How his strong throat moved and his eyes crinkled at the corners. "Dear God. Evelyn Montrose cook a holiday dinner?" He wagged his index finger back and forth. "No, no, dear," he said, jaw clenched in a faux upper crust accent. "One does not cook for the holidays. One has it catered. So much better to be able to speak with your guest, you see." He'd turned a little Thurston Howell III at the end, and for a second I thought he might call me Lovey.

"I see. Of course. What *was* I thinking?"

His grin stayed, but the fakeness dropped away. "It was—what did they call it—a standing rib roast."

"Sounds fancy. Was it good?"

"Of course it was good. Evelyn wouldn't serve anything but the best." There wasn't bitterness in his voice, but I wondered if there had once been when describing his mother. Certainly Aidan in *Folly* had secretly loathed the pretentiousness of his parents, even while enjoying all the perks of being well-off.

Had Montrose done so as well?

He'd said in numerous interviews that Aidan Colly was not Billy Montrose, but the outward similarities were numerous. Maybe he hadn't even seen it himself.

Having read the book so many times, and now seeing a glimpse of Montrose himself… No. I couldn't think like that. They were not the same.

He talked while I ate, taking sips from a beer every now and then. It felt oddly like we were sitting across from each other at a restaurant or something. And the conversation had that feel too, talking about mundane things, not about his work.

I followed his lead, not wanting to bring up Rachel/Esme, and run the risk of being relegated back to intermittent texts, not this wonderful FaceTiming. Because as much as a tiny thrill ran through me when his text tone went off, seeing his face as he spoke only to me, was waaaaay better.

No sharing him with the rest of the class. No wondering if his eyes would turn to me. No shifting my glance at Jane to see if she was flashing him "do me" eyes.

"Oh, my God, that was so amazing," I said as I finished eating. "Thank you again. You really didn't have to do that."

He waved my objection away with a hand and I saw a flash of red on his arm. I'd never seen him wearing red before, not much of any color—he was a black/grey/white wearer mostly. "No problem. If you're working for me on Christmas—" He held up a hand to stop my coming interruption. "And I know that's your choice, that I'm not making you." I relaxed. "Then the least I can do is feed you."

"Well, thank you. It was really great. And I think I have enough leftovers to last me until New Year's." He laughed, but I wasn't far from the truth.

We sat for a moment just looking at each other. I desperately wanted to reach out my hand and touch the screen, but knew it wasn't appropriate, nor would it satisfy this building need I had to touch him ever since he'd sat so close to me on the edge of this very desk.

His eyes moved to the top of his laptop and I realized he was checking the time. My heart started beating more quickly as I searched for a way to keep him online, keep being able to see his gorgeous face. Maybe I should talk about work? I might piss him off, but at least he'd stay with me.

I hated that I'd just had that thought. It kind of reminded me of how I'd felt on Sunday at the mall, standing in front of the display of combat boots.

"Well, I guess I better get going," he said.

"You probably have to be somewhere," I said, though there was just a tiny hint of question in my voice at the end.

"Yeah, well sort of. I've got this thing…"

A lump formed in my throat, but I shoved it down and just smiled and nodded at him. "Uh-huh."

"It's just a group…they're my guy friends from Brown. One of them is getting married next week."

"Oh, a bachelor party? That sounds like fun." It actually sounded like some lucky stripper getting to grind herself all over Montrose while I sat in his chair and had my third eggroll. I swiveled a little in the old wooden chair. It was comfy with its worn leather seat, but the slatted wooden arms curved around—totally inappropriate for a lap dance. But then, giving my boss a lap dance in his office chair wouldn't be real appropriate either. Not that I'd ever given a lap dance.

But I'd certainly be willing to with Montrose.

"No, the bachelor party is this weekend. And I'm not even sure I'm going to that. This is just a quiet thing. Just a few of us having a couple of drinks. Oh, and cigars. Someone said there would be brandy and cigars. I guess we're trying to prove we're grown up now."

"Well, one of you is getting married. Isn't that proving that you're grown up enough?"

He grinned—God, how I loved when he did that. "I will definitely make that point. Maybe it will be argument enough to get us out of the brandy and cigar thing and we can just go to a bar and have a beer."

"That sounds much better to me."

"Yeah, me too." He looked at the clock on his laptop again. "Listen, I wanted to mention something about the last time we actually talked."

Oh, shit. That's why he wanted to FaceTime…he was going to fire me. The dinner was probably my parting gift. "Listen, I'm so sorry for overstepping. I was just caught up in the work. *Your* work. Definitely your work and I won't ever—"

"Syd," he said loudly, cutting me off. I realized he'd said my name several times as I'd rambled on, fighting for my job. Though it somehow felt like I was fighting for more. "Stop," he said more gently, his hands up in a "calm down" gesture. "You didn't overstep." He ran his hand through his hair, tousling it more. And yep, definitely wearing something red. "Or, maybe you did. But if you did, I thank you for it."

I sat back in the chair, not able to hide my relief. But he felt further away from me, so I leaned onto the desk again, dragging my elbow into an open soy sauce packet. I didn't even care, and just nudged it away. "Seriously?" I tentatively asked.

He nodded. "Seriously. Why I wanted to talk about it was because of how I reacted to it."

"You were fine on the phone," I pointed out.

He sat back a little. "I know. I loved talking about it all with you."

"I did too."

"But after I got off the phone, the little insecure writer on my shoulder started whispering to me."

"What did he say?" I asked, fascinated. Was the little guy on his shoulder similar to the one that sat on my shoulder at the mall that same day? And, let's face it, pretty much all the time.

He waved a hand. "Oh, the usual. 'I don't know what I'm doing. *Folly* was a fluke, never to happen again.'"

"You don't believe him, do you?"

He put his hand down, got very still, looked directly into the camera. Directly at me. "I didn't when I was on the phone with you," he said softly.

I knew that I needed to say the right thing. Something about him believing in himself, and not listening to the asshole on his shoulder. But instead, I leaned closer and looked at the camera and said very quietly, "Then don't stop calling me."

He just stared at me with those grey eyes, and I felt like I was at a major fork in the road of my life. And that I wasn't the one who got to choose which path to take. As I held my breath, he slowly—sooo slowly—nodded his head once. "I won't," he said in nearly a whisper.

"Good," I mouthed back, not even able to get the word out.

I saw his shoulder move and it seemed like he wanted to reach out to the screen as I had wanted to earlier. He caught himself as he looked at his moving arm. "Oh, right," he said. "The reason I wanted to FaceTime. I wanted to show you what my mother gave me for Christmas." He tilted his screen so I could see—finally—all of him and not just his face and the ceiling. (Not that there was anything wrong with that face!)

I burst out laughing when I saw that he wore the ugliest Christmas sweater I'd ever seen. "Like, as a joke, right? She gave that to you as a joke? Because you're all going to an ugly Christmas sweater party or something?"

He was laughing too, as he watched me crack up. He held

out the sweater so I could see all of the crazy, geometric, green and red design. "No. Not a joke. At least not to her. She gave my sister one similar to this, but for a girl. She was mortified to wear it to her boyfriend's parents' place tonight, but you could tell my mother loved them and expected us to wear them."

"I mean...seriously?" I knew the sweater was probably from some fancy designer and most likely cost more than four pairs of combat boots, but cost did not always necessarily equate to good taste. And in this case. Uh...no. Just...no.

He laughed again, then got out of his chair, tilted the laptop more and did a pirouette in front of the camera so I could see the back of it, which wasn't any better than the front. Though I didn't really notice it—not with his ass looking so great in his jeans.

"Good luck with the guys wearing that thing," I said.

"I know. I'm going to take such shit from them," he said, still smiling as he sat back in his chair. "The things we do for our mothers, right?"

I just nodded, but didn't say anything. Five years ago I had stopped trying to do anything that would please my mother.

She didn't deserve it.

Shaking off the thought, I said, "Well, you better go and take your share of shit."

His grin died a little as he nodded. He reached for the keyboard, probably to disconnect, then pulled his hand back. "Hey, Syd?"

"Yes?"

He took a deep breath, looked down, and then back up at me. "The sweater wasn't the real reason I wanted to FaceTime instead of call."

"No?" I said, thinking that maybe he had intended to fire me after all.

"No," he said. "I really...*really*...wanted to see you."

I literally could not speak. I finally just nodded and mouthed, "Me too." He smiled a small, almost sad, smile and then he was gone.

I stared at the blank screen for a long time.

NINE

✦

DOES YOUR ROOMMATE JANE *have a boyfriend?* He texted me on Saturday.

No FaceTime. No phone call. A text. About Jane being single.

Shit.

And it'd been so great video chatting with him the past couple of days. Yesterday I even picked my laptop up and moved it around the office, showing him the different piles and what they represented, even going through a couple of the piles and showing how everything had been sorted by date and character.

And we'd spent as much time talking about things other than his book. Like…well, *other* writers' books.

But it had been great. And now he was asking if Jane was single. Via text?

I was half tempted to text that she indeed was very serious with some Bribury guy and was head over heels in love—her flirting with him just being a big joke to her. But I didn't.

No. No boyfriend. She's very single.

She and I had trolled some parties looking for guys, but she wasn't interested in anybody. And anybody I was, didn't seem interested in me—at least not for more than a one-night stand.

Well, she's gonna have a boyfriend now. Or, at least for tonight.

My phone almost dropped from my hand. Jane was with Montrose? Was he in Baltimore, or was she in New York? And Montrose was finally going to cave?

Is she? I texted back. Vague. Noncommittal. Not too prying. *You're with her?* I couldn't resist adding.

Yes. Well, not WITH her, but she's here. And some guy just planted one on her on the dance floor.

Dance floor? She was clubbing in Manhattan? And getting kissed in the middle of a dance floor? I knew anything was possible with Jane, but, still.

I'm at a wedding she's at. A wedding she's in, actually.

Oh, right. Her half sister's wedding.

You're at Betsy Stratton's wedding?

Yes. I went to Brown with her and Jason. He's the guy who we went for drinks with on Christmas night.

Somewhere in the back of my mind I knew that Billy Montrose had been friends at Brown with Betsy Stratton, but I hadn't known Jane then, hadn't known of the weird connection Jane had with the Stratton family, so had never put it together.

Is her dress hideous? She was afraid the dress was going to be God awful.

Shoot. I shouldn't have asked that. I didn't want him studying how good or bad Jane looked. Unless the dress truly was hideous and she looked like a hot mess.

A second ago her guy was twirling her, and she seemed to like the dress just fine. Was smiling ear-to-ear.

Jane?

Haha. That's what I thought. But yep, she's here. I knew about her of course, through Betsy, but was surprised to see she was a bridesmaid. I didn't think she and Bets were that close.

They're not. It's a long story. Jane didn't even want to be there.

Well she's looking pretty happy dancing with this guy.

That was part of the deal she'd made—Jane looking happy to be there, playing the part of loving sister. But maybe it was more than her fulfilling her part of the bargain?

Do you know who the guy is? I figured he might be another college buddy that Montrose went to school with, seeing as both the bride and groom were Brown grads.

No. Never saw him before. He's younger than my group. Looks a little older than Jane. Wearing a tux. And a short ponytail.

Ponytail? I just could not imagine Jane happily dancing at her sister's wedding and kissing a guy with a ponytail.

Open bar, I assume? I asked, trying to find some sense in all this.

You just made me choke on my cocktail. Yes, open bar. But she looks fine, not drunk. Earlier she was dancing with her father and then with some old windbag, long time senator.

Wow. She is toeing the line for sure.

Maybe. Not so sure Grayson Spaulding was happy about the kiss. He and Caro Stratton have been watching the happy couple.

Betsy and Jason?

No, Jane and Ponytail.

I was just about to ask him to video tape them dancing and send it to me, so I could see for myself, but before I could he texted, *Gotta go. My chance to dance with Betsy.*

Okay.

Wish we could have FaceTimed instead.

Me too. I'll bet you look amazing in a tux I wanted to type, but had the good sense not to.

Talk to you tomorrow.

Bye.

And he was gone. I spent another few minutes working, but my concentration was shot. Thoughts of Jane dancing and kissing a mystery man kept me entertained for the whole walk back to my dorm.

Thoughts of Montrose in a tux kept me on edge for the entire night.

"How was the wedding last night?" I asked Jane when I called her the next morning.

There was a pause. A pause in which a thousand scenarios went through my head. The worst one being that Montrose and Betsy had run into Jane and Ponytail on the dance floor, decided to switch partners and had realized during the three-minute song how much they'd been fighting their mutual attraction, and decided to finally act on it.

I think maybe I'd been surrounded by story-telling notes for too long.

"It was…bearable."

"And the dress? Was it as bad as you feared?"

"Well, it was peach, and there was lace involved."

I started giggling, as did she. "You know what," she said, "it actually wasn't *that* bad. It looked okay on me. And it twirled nicely when I danced."

"Did you dance a lot?"

"No. Not much. Some old goat got a little touchy feely and I only danced for a little bit after that."

"Yuck. Did you put the goat in his place?"

She laughed a tiny bit. "Sort of. Had to play it carefully because he's some kind of influential guy for my father's party."

"Why does that matter?"

"Because—get this—my father's going to run for governor of Maryland."

Jane's father had been a presidential candidate years ago, but had dropped out of the race when his mistress (Jane's mom) had become pregnant (with Jane). He'd been out of politics ever since.

"Are you shitting me?" I asked.

"I wish."

We talked about her dad and his upcoming election for half an hour. How they wanted Jane to be involved and how she could use that to her advantage.

If her father was half the bargaining mastermind that Jane was, Maryland might be in good hands with him as governor.

She never said anything about seeing Montrose at the wedding. And she definitely didn't say anything about kissing a guy with a ponytail.

We said our goodbyes. It was Sunday. I had planned to go to Montrose's for the whole day since I wasn't working for my admin job. After breakfast at the nearly empty caf, instead of walking on to Snyder Hall, I turned around and went back to my dorm room. The snow was falling, getting my new boots wet. I hadn't worn a warm enough sweater under my coat and the idea of crawling back into bed and reading the day away was more tempting than spending the day with Rachel/Esme. That realization alone made me admit I needed a break, and indeed went back to the dorm, put on some heavy wool socks, some sweats, another sweater, and bundled up in bed with my comforter around me like a burrito.

Okay if I take the day off? I texted to Montrose. I really didn't think he'd care. I just wanted an excuse to start a conversation.

Of course I don't mind. I can't believe you've been in that office every day. I've told you that you didn't have to be.

He had. Several times. And I'd always argued back that I *wanted* to be there as much as I was. Which was true.

But today I needed to recharge. And I always did that best with a good book.

Okay, good. Thanks. I'll be back there after my admin shift tomorrow.

Take tomorrow off too, if you want. You're way ahead of where I thought you'd be.

Nope. Just need a day to lay in bed and read, you know?
Oh yeah, I know. I know very well.

He was a writer, and also a voracious reader. Of course he knew.

TEN

THE NEXT DAY, MONDAY, I was recharged from a day in bed reading the newest John Irving novel, and couldn't wait to get back to Montrose's office. But first I had to get through my shift testing faux grading in the new front end system.

One of the consultants asked what I was doing for New Year's Eve. The consultants, most from the firm's Texas office, were here for the holidays too. They'd flown home for the long Christmas weekend, but apparently they would not be doing the same for New Year's.

I told the guy I didn't know of anything going on.

"No, that's not what I meant," he said. "I was asking if *you* were doing anything. And if not…would you like to?"

I stared at him. He was pretty hot and we'd done a little good-natured joking when we'd been working in the same areas. But something made me tell him no.

Okay, it wasn't just "something" and I knew it. It was Montrose.

Which was totally stupid, and also… Yeah, stupid was definitely the best word for it.

It wasn't like there was anything between us. And yet, there kind of was.

It wasn't like he wouldn't be out with someone on New Year's Eve. And yet, I somehow thought he wouldn't be.

It wasn't like I'd be spending it with him. And yet, maybe I would be…at least virtually.

A girl could—foolishly, completely inappropriately—hope.

The consultant took the rejection in stride and I got the feeling that he was a co-ed in every port kind of guy.

When I got to Montrose's office in the late afternoon I stopped cold as soon as I opened the door.

He had been here. I knew it, though everything looked the same. It was just—okay, this is really hokey—the air was different.

I looked at my well-thought-out piles of his notes. They hadn't been moved or jostled from the precarious perches some of them maintained. But I knew he'd looked through them.

I circled around the desk and my breath caught as I saw a note right in the center. And definitely not one I'd written.

Sorry I missed you. I was in Chesney for that wedding so stayed at my place. I didn't want you to get out of bed (or book) yesterday, so I didn't mention that I'd be stopping in. The notes are in great shape, organized much better than I could have done. And just seeing them would have sent me off on more note-taking tangents, so it's great that you were able to do them for me.

Can't thank you enough.

Billy

I dropped into the creaky, wooden desk chair. Unfuckingbelievable. I'd missed him because I'd wanted to stay in bed and read on a snowy Sunday afternoon. Something I could have done any Sunday—in fact, did *most* Sundays.

I looked at the note again, this time noticing the small postscript at the very bottom of the piece of paper.

I miss you—is that crazy?

Just as I was thinking how un-crazy that was, my phone rang with his tone. Knowing I couldn't get my laptop out and booted fast enough, I answered the FaceTime call on my phone.

"I just got here," I said, out of breath, like I'd run all the way here from the admin building, when in reality, I was just gasping from the absurdity of our near miss.

And then chastising myself for feeling that way. I worked for him. Next week I'd be seeing him all the time.

The thought of seeing him more than just three times a week for a very short hour got my breath going all the more quickly.

He chuckled a little. "That eager to get to work? That you'd run to the office?" But he seemed to know that it wasn't physical exertion that had my cheeks red and my chest rising. Not that he'd even see my chest with me holding my phone so closely to my face.

The better to see you with, my dear.

I didn't even bother to explain my out-of-breathness. "You were here?" I said, trying to control my voice. Shit, it almost cracked.

Get it together, Syd. You are going to see this guy every day, you can't let him know what he does to you.

But he knew. And what's more, he seemed a little flushed too.

"I actually thought you'd still be at your other job," he said.

"Nope. Like I said, I just got here. They had us stop a little early today because they found a bug or glitch or something that they wanted to look at."

"Oh," he said. Nothing else, but he looked slightly embarrassed.

"Why would you call if you thought I was at the admin job?"

"Nothing. I mean…" he let out a big sigh, ran his hand over his sexy stubble like he was noting it for the first time.

"Did you already see the note—yeah, of course you did."

I nodded, not saying anything.

"I just thought…Christ, I don't know what I thought. I was just going to tell you to trash it without reading it, but…shit…even saying it out loud sounds stupid. As if you'd not look at something I wrote to you just because I asked you not to."

The funny thing was, I probably wouldn't look. Well, okay, maybe. Yeah, definitely.

I kept my mouth shut.

He sighed again. "Well, listen, I have to go. My parents and I are going out for dinner and we 'simply can't miss our reservation, darling.'" Thurston Howell had returned.

"Okay," I said. "I'm just going to organize the last of it tonight and put it in to the order I want to transcribe from. I'll start that fresh tomorrow, so I probably won't be here that long tonight."

"I most likely won't have my phone on during dinner, so just text with any questions, and I'll get to them as soon as I can."

"Will do. But I don't think I'll have any questions, I'm in the homestretch with this part."

"Well…" He looked down, opened his mouth to say something, then shut it. Looking up, he finally said, "I guess… good night."

"Okay." I started to move my thumb to the "end" button, but stopped. "Billy?" I said, I think using only his first name to him for the first time. Maybe I had that first day in his office when he'd hired me. But it was different this time.

"Yes?"

"It isn't crazy," I said softly. "I miss you, too."

He smiled softly, then more widely. "Night, Syd," he said, and then disconnected.

ELEVEN

❖

"AND THEN JASON LEFT, and we knew we were destined to end the night in the drunk tank…which we did."

I laughed at Montrose's story of his most wild New Year's Eve. Fitting, because we were FaceTiming on New Year's Eve itself. We had given up the pretense of it being about work and I'd just taken his call in my room, snuggled up in bed, the snow falling outside my window, the glow of a strictly forbidden candle illuminating me just enough for him to see.

The light from my laptop was making him seem almost ethereal in my darkened room.

"Come on, your turn," he said for the thirtieth time since we'd started our conversation.

I was wearing pajama bottoms and a cami, but it was so cool in the room that I had pulled on a baby-blue rag wool sweater that Jane had once left in my room and so I had—naturally—taken possession of it.

It was both scratchy and soft, looked about fifty years old, and was something I would never wear out of my dorm room (though Jane did, of course), but it had become my go-to sweater if I was just hanging in the room.

Somehow I felt…braver by wearing it in front of Montrose, even though it was nearly covered up by my comforter and the angle at which my laptop lay, wedged on my raised knees and thighs.

"No," I said, also for about the thirtieth time since we'd started. "You tell another one. You're the storyteller after all."

"You don't have to be a writer to tell a story about past New Year's Eves. Just pick one."

"But you have *so* many more to choose from than I do."

He grinned and—corny as it sounds—my heart literally skipped a beat. "Ooh, was that an old man dig? Need I remind you that I'm still under thirty?"

"And yet still an old man to me," I teased, then wished I hadn't when I saw his grin slowly vanish from his face.

"Yeah, there is that," he said.

I started shaking my head, feeling my hair sliding on the pillow propped beneath me. "I'm kidding. It's not an issue. At least not for me."

He watched me for a long time, like he was looking for a tell or something that I might be lying. "Honestly," I added.

It was weird, discussing obstacles to our relationship, when, well, there was no relationship. Not really. Not yet.

But the more we talked, the more we laughed, the more we looked meaningfully at each other as we said good night… Yeah, there was something there, even if it was undefined at this point, even to us. *Especially* to us.

But so there would be no objection that he could obsess about (did guys even obsess like we girls did?), I drove the point home. "I'm nineteen, almost twenty. I was old for my class." A little lie, but he didn't need to know I had missed nearly all of eighth grade and needed to repeat it. "And, let's face it, I've probably lived more of a life growing up where I did, than most of these other freshman girls."

Reminding him I was a student probably wasn't the smartest tactic, but after a while he just smiled and said, "So, since you've got all this life experience, your turn to share a story. New Year's Eve or not." I opened my mouth to argue, but he quickly added, "I feel like I've done all the talking."

I shook my head. "No. And even if you have, I've enjoyed it."

Just as I was about to argue more, a roar went up from outside on his end, loud enough for us both to hear. "Jesus, it's almost midnight already," he said. The sound now became a discernible countdown. "When did we start chatting?"

"Around eight," I said. It had been exactly 8:03, but who was counting?

He turned his head toward his window, then got out of his chair and picked up his laptop. "You can't see Times Square from here, but we'll be able to hear it," he said walking with his laptop—with me—out onto a terrace that seemed to span the entire length of his parents' apartment.

"Wow," I said, getting a touch of sea sickness as he moved the laptop around, finding the best place to settle, which apparently was a table and chairs set of some type. "You have a terrace door in your *bedroom*? Soooo Upper East Side."

He shrugged. "Yeah, it is nice. But you should see *my* apartment. No terrace. No rooftop pool. None of that shit. It's totally starving artist."

But he wasn't starving, had never starved, never really struggled. According to "Forbes," royalties from *Folly* still topped the mid six figures even five years after publication.

Yeah, Montrose didn't know what a true starving artist was.

It was darker outside, but a light was on further down the terrace behind him. They had reached the final ten seconds by the time he'd sat and had me steady.

(Like I was *ever* steady in his presence!)

"Explain again why you're here with me and not down

there?" I said, meaning Manhattan in general, Times Square in particular.

"God, the thought," he said, doing a mock shudder. "You're from New York, you know what a zoo it is on this night. I guarantee you, ninety percent of the people out there tonight, at least in Times Square, are tourists."

"We are *not* both from New York. At least not the same New York."

He waved a hand of dismissal, his white cotton buttoned-down shirt looking ghostly in the dark of the night. "Yeah, yeah, you're a Queens girl. Whatever. You've been to the city."

Not often. I was usually saddled with my little brothers and there was no way I was going to lug them into Manhattan. "Yeah, you're right. Smarter to stay in tonight," I said, hoping to curb the "my Manhattan/your Manhattan" direction the conversation was headed. He didn't need to know about *my* New York.

I was trying hard to forget. To become a Bribury Basic and let the Queens girl fall away.

He looked like he was going to pursue it. I felt my lips tighten, like I was preparing to keep my secrets, and he sat back in his chair. The light behind him created a halo effect around him, and the screen's illumination washed him out, creating this kind of angel-like presence.

Yeah, I had idolized Montrose since I was fourteen, but even I knew the guy was no angel.

He laced his fingers together across his chest, resting his elbows on the wrought-iron arms of the chair. I couldn't see it, but from his movements I could tell that he'd stretched out his legs.

"So," he said, "any resolutions? Goals for the new year?"

I relaxed, my lips untightening. He was going to let it go.

I was going to tell him about the thing Lily, Jane and I did with the envelope sealing, but I didn't. For one thing, it kind of felt like I'd be betraying Jane and Lily by telling him about it. Like, it was something that belonged to just the three of us. And, even though I didn't know what they'd written, even talking about doing it, was somehow spilling a secret.

Secondly, I didn't want to put the thought of Jane in his head. Oh, I was past the point of thinking Montrose would succumb to Jane's flirtations, and it seemed that Jane was beyond Montrose, too, due to the ponytailed guy, and the dance floor kissing. But…still.

Lastly, I didn't bring up our envelopes because I didn't want Montrose to ask what I'd written down and sealed up for a year.

It had been the night before Montrose had hired me, and my New Year's statement now seemed childish and…well, freshman-like, even though it had just been two weeks earlier.

"I guess I hadn't really thought about it," I said. It wasn't exactly a lie. The thing Lily, Jane and I did wasn't exactly resolutions.

In the background I could hear the final countdown, and the roar which meant…yep, I checked the time on my laptop…it was now the new year.

Montrose's head tilted in the direction of Times Square, but his eyes stayed on the screen. "Happy New Year, Syd," he said softly.

"Happy New Year, Billy."

I licked my lips, like I was expecting the lauded kiss at midnight, but that was stupid. What? We were going to each press our lips against our laptop screens? Like an inmate getting a visit in prison and kissing his wife through the glass that separated them?

There was no way my first kiss with Montrose was going to taste like MacBook Air.

Not that there would necessarily *be* a first kiss.

God, I hoped there would be a first kiss. And a second, and…infinity.

He sat forward in his chair and I held my breath. He looked at me for a long time, seemingly studying my face as if he would later be asked to describe me for a police sketch artist or something. Opening his mouth to say something, he changed his mind and gave his head a tiny shake, then sat back in the chair.

"So, back to resolutions. You said you hadn't thought about it. Now's your chance. What do you resolve for this next year?"

"Umm…let me think," I said, my mind whooshing over thoughts and ideas of things that would be okay to tell him. "Do you have any?" I finally said.

He waved a hand of dismissal. "That's easy. Write and finish my next book."

"Oh, yeah, of course. That's a good one. A great one, actually."

Another wave, this one smaller, his wrist barely rising above the arm of his chair. "Sure, but it's been the same resolution for the past five years."

"Yeah, but you know what you have now, that you didn't for the past five years?"

"Insight? Drive? Maturity? Discipline? Yeah, no. I'm pretty sure I still don't have any of those."

"You have me," I said, smiling, almost laughing, letting him know I was teasing. But damn, I would absolutely love for the organizing and transcribing I was doing for him to be the catalyst for him to keep his resolution.

"Do I?" he said, almost in a whisper.

"Do you what?"

He leaned all the way forward, resting his forearms on the

table, right in front of the laptop. So close I could make out the grey of his eyes, even in the poor light.

"Do I…have you?" he asked.

I didn't hesitate. "Yes," I answered, "you do."

His shoulders drooped a little and I realized they'd been bunched up…tensed up…while he'd asked me that question.

Could he honestly doubt how I felt about him?

Well, yeah, maybe. Because he didn't know what he'd meant to me for the past five years. He only thought we had *shared* the past two weeks.

But maybe even that alone should have let him know I would be anything he wanted me to be.

I had molded myself into a Bribury Basic, I could easily become what would appeal to Billy Montrose.

Jane's pendant seemed to burn against my skin just then, and I pulled it out from beneath the comfy sweater, feeling the warmth from my skin as I held it, tracing my fingers along the outside curves.

Strength. I had it, I should show it, Jane had said about the necklace.

I pushed the thought away as Montrose said, "Do you think we should talk about what's going to happen when the semester starts?"

"What do you mean?"

He shifted uncomfortably in his seat and I dropped the pendant out of my hands, then held on tighter to the sides of my laptop. Was he already backpedaling?

"What, *specifically*, do you mean?"

"Well, I mean, you're not *my* student anymore, but you are still *a* student."

"Yes…"

He rubbed his hand across his stubbled chin. "And you are my employee."

"A short-term, project-specific employee. I mean, I'm not going to be in a position to cry sexual harassment because you didn't promote me when I deserved it."

"Not that I wouldn't. Give you the promotion, I mean."

I smiled, and he returned it, his teeth almost as bright and evident as his white shirt. "I know you would," I said.

His smile stayed as he said, "So…apart from you being a student and my employee…absolutely no roadblocks for us to…"

"To…?"

"Well, I guess that's the question, isn't it?"

I tried to channel my future, super-confident, twenty-eight-year-old self. "Do you really think it's a question anymore?"

The smile left his face as I just looked at him, then silently quirked one brow up in…question? Challenge?

Slowly…oh, so slowly…he shook his head just the tiniest amount. But it was enough for me to silently thank my future self for being so bold.

"No," he said almost too quietly for me to hear. In fact, maybe I'd just read his lips and hadn't even heard him at all.

It didn't matter. I had the answer I wanted. I nodded once but didn't say anything. I would have given anything to be with him in person at that moment, sitting on his terrace, hearing revelers from the streets below and out in the city. To be able to reach across the table and touch him. To get up and walk over to him, where he'd make room for me on his lap. And I'd wrap my arms around him, feeling the thin, cool cotton fabric of his shirt, and the hard, warm man beneath.

Wait. The cotton of his shirt? "You must be freezing out there," I said, realizing he'd been outside for the last ten minutes or more with no coat, hat or gloves. I shivered in my warm cozy bed just thinking about it.

"Actually," he said, grinning, "I am totally freezing my

nuts off out here."

"Why didn't you go back inside? After midnight?"

He shrugged and I noticed the redness of his cheeks and nose. "I was going to right after the countdown, but it seemed like, I don't know, the darkness and stillness out here gave us a deeper level of…intimacy."

"Wow, spoken like a writer. Yeah, you better finish that book this year, so you're not spouting lines like that in everyday conversation."

He laughed, then turned his head. "You're right. I hear my parents coming in. I should probably go see how their night was."

"They braved the madness?"

"Not really. Our neighbors a couple of floors down had a small party. They didn't even have to leave the building."

He started to rise and I felt a moment of panic, the same feeling I got every time one of our conversations was winding up.

"Umm…okay, well, I'll be in the office tomorrow if—"

He was shaking his head as he rose from the table and picked up his laptop. "We leave tomorrow for Gstaad to ski for a week. My parents, sister, her boyfriend and me."

I didn't bother starting in on *my* New York not remotely being a launching pad for a European vacation. But I thought it.

"Have fun," I said, keeping all traces of jealousy out of my voice, though I wasn't really sure who, or what, I was jealous of. I didn't even ski. (Just the thought of someone from my neighborhood on skis made me inwardly cringe.)

"Thanks, I will. But I probably won't be calling you while I'm gone. Time zone, and I didn't get the roam thing for my phone. There's always internet in the resort, for email, but…"

I didn't want him to think he had to be accountable to me.

Waving a hand, I said, "Don't worry about it. I have plenty to keep me busy for the next week and a half. Any questions can wait until you get back."

He nodded while closing the terrace door behind him and stepped back into his bedroom, which was about the size of my family's entire apartment. "Yeah, I know you can handle it," he said.

"Okay. Well, then…"

"Hey, Syd?"

"Yeah?"

"Do you think it's going to be weird, be awkward, when we see each other for the first time?"

"You mean like a blind date or something?"

He chuckled, setting his laptop down on the desk, but continuing to stand. He tilted it so I could see his face, but being eye level with his body was very nice indeed.

"I guess. I mean, we've grown…really close over the past two weeks, and yet…"

"And yet…"

We watched each other, neither one wanting to define the other's feelings—or their own—by finishing the sentence. He rubbed his chin again. "I just don't want it to be awkward, you know?"

"It won't," I said. I hoped.

We wished each other "Happy New Year" again, and then hung up.

I placed my laptop on the floor by my bed and wrapped myself tighter in my comforter. With my computer light off, the candlelight took over and I lay there and thought about the upcoming year, and how much I couldn't wait for the next week and a half to fly by.

This was going to be the best year of my life, I just knew it.

TWELVE

MUCH LIKE MONTROSE HAD FEARED, it was awkward when we first saw each other. For about ten seconds.

And then he kissed me.

I was sitting at his desk typing up notes when I heard his key in the door. I always kept the door locked when I was in there alone.

I knew he'd arrived home from Switzerland yesterday— he'd texted me that he was on US soil, but hadn't mentioned when he'd be coming back to Bribury. It was Saturday, and students were beginning to arrive, though most would be coming back tomorrow, with the new semester starting on Monday.

I guess I really hadn't expected him to arrive until Sunday night, and that I wouldn't see him until Monday afternoon.

I rose from my seat as the door unlocked, and moved around the desk as he opened and closed it.

A slow smile crept across his ruggedly handsome face as he saw me. "I knew you'd be here," he said as he tossed his messenger bag onto the now box-free guest chair.

"I'm here," I stated the obvious as he looked at me.

"Me too, now," he said. The awkward level rose a few decibels until he laughed and stepped the five paces to get to me, put his hands—still cold from the outdoors and not wearing gloves—on my face, and brought his lips to mine.

Though he was cold from being outside, his lips were warm and the feel of them on mine nearly burned, the intensity was so strong. I had loved this man for five years, never thinking I would ever even meet him. I was in awe of his talent for so long. To now have his hands on my face, stroking my chin with his thumb as he ran his tongue along the seam of my lips...it was beyond my comprehension.

It had been the stuff of dreams, of fantasies, and yet here he was, kissing me. The feel of his camel hair coat as I placed my hands on his elbows, bent so that his hands could touch me. Real.

The scent of his cologne, barely there, but deep and musky, and not at all like the preppy Burberry Brit that Bribury guys bathed in. Real.

The taste of coffee as I opened my mouth to him and he swept his tongue in to find mine, to dance together. Real.

And yet, so...surreal.

Sliding my hands up his arms, I stepped closer to him, desperate to feel his body against mine.

"Syd," he whispered against my lips. "God, I missed you."

All I could do was nod a tiny bit because his mouth covered mine again. More pressure this time, more urgency. His hands fell away from my face and he pulled me into his arms. I wrapped my arms around him, my hands sliding through the hair at the back of his head—so soft and wavy, maybe even a little wet. Was it snowing outside? I burrowed my fingers deeper, and the backs of my knuckles encountered more wetness. Definitely melting snow.

It seemed like steam rose from the contact of my warm hands in his cold and wet hair, but maybe that was just how I was feeling inside. Very hot and steamy, like I was being singed by extreme weather conditions.

Being singed by Montrose.

I could feel his breath against my cheek as he angled his mouth for a better, deeper position. His hands slid down my fleece, and curved around my butt, pulling me even closer to him. His chest was strong and solid, and I loved that he was a man and not a Bribury boy who was still growing into himself.

I needed to feel that chest, know for sure how solid, how *real*, he was. But there were too many layers on him. I slid my hands down the lapels of this smooth-as-silk camel-hair coat and pushed it off his shoulders, his hands quickly returning to my butt once his coat had dropped to the floor.

Being Saturday, he wasn't wearing a sports coat, but instead had on a three-quarter zip wool sweater in black with the soft cotton of a grey T-shirt peeking out at the collar.

One of his hands glided up from my butt and underneath my fleece, pulled my cami from my jeans and crept onto the small of my back.

Yes, that was what I needed, too—to touch his bare skin. "Yes," was what I murmured against his mouth. Yes, was what I would always tell him. He squeezed my ass and his hand at my back flattened against my skin, and he pulled me closer.

I'd be tucked into him with no room to move, except my hands were skimming his chest, then moved down to the bottom of his sweater. I raised the sweater just a tiny bit, then dipped a finger into the waistband of his jeans, right at the button, feeling both the harsh denim and the soft cotton of his tucked-in tee.

His breath hitched and he gently bit down on my lower lip, causing a groan from both of us. I slowly moved my finger back and forth, though no deeper into his jeans. "Jesus," he said against my cheek as he kissed me there. Moving to my jaw, and down my neck, he placed kisses all along the way. Some soft, barely there, and very sweet. Others long and involved sucking, and weren't sweet at all. I loved it all, baring my neck for him, his nose nudging the high collar of my fleece pullover out of the way.

I was just about to end the teasing (though the teasing was pretty damn good) and slide my hand lower, when a knock at the door pulled me out of it. It was a good thing, too, because Montrose kept reaching for me, even as I stepped away and returned to my side of the desk.

A look of confusion—perhaps even devastation?—crossed his face until a second knock came and he visibly shook his head.

He used to do that in class sometimes, pulling his thoughts back to us, back to reality.

I always wondered what he'd been thinking about when he did that.

Seeing the hunger in his eyes, the depth of it sending chills down throughout my limbs as I sat down behind the desk, didn't have me wondering what he'd been thinking this time.

He'd been thinking we were about thirty seconds away from pulling each other's clothes off, and ruining all my hard organizational work by swiping the credenza clear and laying me on it.

And I'd be so okay with replacing every last scrap of paper in its rightful place...*after*.

With a sigh, and a look of regret—and promise—he turned from me, grabbed his coat from the floor, and returned to the door, opening it just as I started typing into my laptop, pretending whoever was at the door was none of my business.

And it wasn't, but whoever it was, they were now firmly at the top of my shit list.

"I *thought* I saw you coming in the building from my office, Billy," came a female voice. I didn't even look up, just kept on typing. I would have been more proud of myself for not being nosy, except that I could tell from her voice that our mood killer was a much older woman. Like, grandma old.

"Hello, Corrine, how were your holidays?" he said, stepping away from the door and allowing in my enemy number one.

Except she couldn't be my enemy number one because, well, she was just adorable. I realized this as she came completely into the office, Montrose shutting the door behind her, still holding his coat firmly in place in front of what I knew to be a pretty impressive hard-on.

Corrine was like a ball of cotton: white, fluffy hair, and nearly as round as she was tall, which was not very.

Totally a nurturer, Corrine, you could tell at first glance.

I briefly thought of my own grandmother. My earliest memory of her was hearing her tell my mother, "Don't bring that spic bastard around here anymore. She don't look like no grandkid of mine." This was the closest I ever came to knowing the ethnicity of my father (the spic slur), and I wasn't even sure that she knew for certain.

I would see her again only when she'd come to visit my redheaded, oh, so Irish, little brothers.

She never acknowledged me, even though it was obvious that I was the one taking care of her beloved little Irish potatoes.

I'd bet my whole paycheck from Montrose that Corrine hugged and kissed every one of her grandkids with the same amount of love and enthusiasm.

"Oh, they were wonderful, Billy, thank you for asking. I went to Chicago and visited my daughter and her family. So wonderful to see those grandchildren, you know they're the only ones that don't live in Maryland anymore."

Montrose was nodding, like he did indeed know where each and every one of Corrine's grandchildren resided. He leaned against the credenza, his fine ass resting just between two different stacks of his notes.

"And then this past week we saw all the ones around here. Which we do quite often, of course, but you know me...I just can't get enough of them."

Yep, Corrine had probably not rung in the new year by calling one of her grandkids "spic bastard." I kept my head down and typed.

"That's great," Montrose said.

"And how about you, Billy? Your family all doing well?"

Out of the corner of my eye I could see the picture on Montrose's desk of his family as he gave Corrine a brief summary of his break.

"And New Year's Eve? Did you go to Times Square?" she asked.

My fingers stilled and I looked up then to find him staring at me. "Uh, no. I spent it in. Just a quiet evening with... someone special."

"Oh, that's wonderful. I suppose to a native New Yorker that gets kind of old."

He just nodded his agreement. Corrine then turned her attention to me. "Oh, I'm sorry," he said. "Corrine, this is my new literary assistant, Sydney O'Brien. Syd, Corrine Patterson. She pretty much runs the department."

She swatted at Montrose in an "Oh, Billy," delightfully exasperated kind of way, as she made her way to me. I stood, and offered my hand to her. "It's nice to meet you, Mrs. Patterson."

"Oh, Corrine is fine, please." Her hand was soft and warm, but the handshake firm.

"Syd," I said, returning her smile.

"It's a pleasure to meet you," she said, and I nodded my agreement. She waved me back to the chair I had just vacated. "Please, dear, don't let me disturb you from your work."

"You didn't," I said, but sat back down anyway, though I

continued to keep my attention on Corrine. And Montrose. Always on Montrose.

"Syd's helping me get all my notes together so I can—hopefully—spend all my time not in class, writing."

There was a momentary look of something that resembled…hurt? on Corrine's face and then she bloomed into a warm smile (I doubt there was any other kind of smile for Corrine). "Well, that's wonderful. And exactly what you need, Billy, so you can finish that book. Everybody's so anxious to read it, and I'll be at the front of the line at the bookstore." She clasped her hands together, as if she couldn't contain her glee at the thought.

My eyes were on Montrose and, though it was slight and Corrine probably wouldn't notice, his body tensed at her words. The black sweater, which I'd had my hands under only moments ago, seemed to pull tighter across his shoulders.

I wasn't sure if it was Corrine assuming that Billy was close to finishing his novel (when I'd just spent three weeks sifting through the evidence that it hadn't even been started), or the crazy anticipation of Corrine, and really, the entire literary world and reading public.

Most likely both, and it was a wonder Corrine didn't pick up on Montrose's lack of enthusiasm as she rambled on about how excited she was to read it, and how certain she was that it would be brilliant.

All lovely sentiments, and though Montrose had a friendly smile on his face for Corrine, even from where I sat I could see his eyes turn that dark and stormy grey that, if I'd been the captain of a boat and saw seas that stormy, I'd turn back and head for safer harbor.

She was about to go even deeper about her love for *Folly*, when Montrose stepped away from the credenza, tossed his coat on the empty chair (Corrine apparently quickly becoming a boner-killer), and cut her off, by motioning to the neatly stacked piles behind him.

"Yes. You can see how helpful Syd has been already, and all this was just over break."

She turned to me, the smile firmly on her face, as if she knew what a pleasure it must have been for me to dig around in Montrose's notes.

She was correct on that count.

"And, I guess I better get ready for Monday's classes," he said, moving to the bookcase in the corner and pulling a binder off the shelf.

"Yes, of course," Corrine said, moving to the door. "It's nice to have you back, Billy."

"It's good to be back," he said, but he was looking at me when he said it. Then he turned more fully to Corrine and said, "And it's really good to see you again, too, Corrine." There was genuine warmth in his voice and Corrine notice it too, because a cute little blush covered her cherubic face.

"Let me know if you need anything—supplies, or that kind of thing," she said to me, then with a wave she was out the door.

Slowly, he stalked the small room toward me, locking the door, and throwing the binder on the chair, it landing on top of his coat.

He came around the side of the desk. "Now," he said as he placed one hand on the arm of my chair, the other on the desk, pinning me in, "where were we?"

THIRTEEN

WE KISSED. AND KISSED. And kissed some more. We moved from me sitting in my chair, to us both standing, to us both sitting on the couch, kissing the whole time.

But, much to my frustration (and, okay, maybe a little relief) all we did was kiss. No more groping for clothes, no more pulling shirts free of jeans.

It seemed like the kisses and groping before Corrine interrupted had taken the frenzied edge off and we were now able to relax and just enjoy…many, many, kisses.

I hadn't been with a guy who just wanted to kiss like that for a long time. Okay, never. It was both refreshing and frustrating.

Yeah, really frustrating.

But I followed his lead, and he never once moved again to remove any of my clothes, or even stick a hand under my fleece, though his hands did tend to gravitate to my ass most of the time.

After at least an hour, (seriously, it had to be over an hour!) he broke away, placing his forehead against mine.

"I've got to go," he whispered.

I pulled back, surprised. I guess I'd assumed if he had come back on Saturday it was so we— No. I couldn't think like that, I couldn't read anything in to his actions—or inactions—

toward me.

He had to make the rules, because he was worried enough about breaking them by just being with me—his employee and a student. "I'm sorry, but I have to go to a thing for the department. Just drinks, but now that Corrine saw me, I can't use the excuse that I hadn't come back in time to go."

"No. Sure. Of course you can't." I tried to hide my disappointment from him, but I was happy to see a smidge of the same feeling on him by the way he eyed my mouth and then let out a long sigh as he rose from the couch.

I packed up and walked out with him, ready to call it a day. I didn't want to be in the office anymore without Montrose. Hell, after making out on the couch (and desk) with him, I probably wouldn't ever want to be in there without him again.

It was dark when we left Snyder Hall, and the snow was falling. Not big, fluffy flakes that would land gracefully on my eyelashes and cheek, causing Montrose to want to gently brush them away as he gazed at me.

No, this was that kind of hard, sleety stuff that seemed to come at us sideways, causing us to keep our heads down and not gaze at anything more than where to place our next footstep.

There were people milling around. Not many, but after three weeks of walking around campus nearly alone, it seemed odd to see so many of my fellow students trudging through the snow.

Montrose took our fellow companions in stride, just bidding me good night, that he'd see me Monday, and heading off in the opposite direction from me.

I hadn't expected a hug and kiss—I knew we could never do anything like that in public.

Still, I walked back to Creyts with a feeling of…not exactly rejection. After all, we'd just spent over an hour proving we wanted very much to be together, in whatever capacity that turned out to be.

I guess I was feeling a sense of uneasy acceptance. A new reality forming for me. If I wanted to be more than just an employee to Montrose (and, oh God, did I), then this was how it would be. Stolen time in his office, scurrying to right ourselves when people dropped in. Him having his own life and social events, me having mine. I suppose it wouldn't set off campus gossip alarms if we had the occasional cup of coffee or slice of pizza in public—I did work for him after all. But that would probably be it, and it wouldn't be too regular.

I saw a lot of Chinese delivery in our future.

I guess it should have added an element of excitement to the idea that Montrose and I were…going to be Montrose and I, and what all that entailed.

The taboo of it all, the secrecy. But honestly, I didn't need the added thrill. I was quite thrilled enough that I would be able to spend a semester in the company of Billy Montrose.

And his kisses.

When I got to my room, I knew immediately from the open doors, the lights and music (something from the seventies) coming from the other side of the suite, that Jane was back.

Sure, Jane and I certainly had our bumps early on, but a warm feeling buzzed through me to know that my suitemate was back. I threw my backpack, coat, beanie and mittens on the empty bed and quickly made my way through the empty bathroom to Lily and Jane's side of the suite.

"Welcome back," I said as I entered, delighted to find not only Jane, but Lily as well.

"Hey," Jane said from her bed, where she was sprawled on her back, phone in hand. She put the phone down and propped herself up with some pillows. "You survived the barren halls of

Bribury. No ghosts?"

I chuckled. "Nope. I made it. It was kind of weird, though."

Lily was standing near her bed, but came over and gave me a hug, then returned to unpacking her bags. "Oh, my God," she said, looking me over. "I got the same boots for Christmas." She pointed at my new combat boots as she held up a pair of her own, pulled from a huge duffle bag on wheels. It looked like Louis Vuitton had gone Army or something.

The inner relief I felt was huge. I had indeed gotten the right pair. Now, I know most girls might have been pissed that they had the same piece of clothing as their roommate, but not me. Not if said roommate was Lily Spaulding, who innately knew the right thing to wear. I would blend with Lily, and thus with Bribury.

"That's random," I said, like I hadn't agonized over getting the right pair only a few weeks ago. I noticed my new boots were leaving small puddles underneath me from the melting snow. I undid them and placed them on the little mat by the door, then went to join Jane, crawling onto the foot of her bed, my back against the wall, my feet hanging over the side. She nudged me with a toe—Jane's version of a big welcome hug—and I squeezed her thick wool sock in reply.

"How long have you guys been here?" I asked.

"I've been here a couple of hours," Jane answered. "Lily just showed up about twenty minutes ago. I was going to text you, but figured you'd be back any minute. Where have you been?"

"I was at work," I answered.

"On Saturday?" Lily asked. She'd finished unpacking, flattening her duffle and sliding it under her bed, then sacked out on her stomach, pulling a pillow under her head and turning on her side to face Jane and me. "Man, that new system must be pretty shaky if they're still doing testing the weekend before classes start."

My mind raced with how much to tell Jane and Lily about my job with Montrose. I didn't want to lie to them, but I was not prepared to talk about even the clerical work I was doing for him, let alone the…other activities he and I had been engaged in.

I wanted to keep it to myself for a while, it felt so new and so fragile. And I wasn't even sure what "it" was.

"Actually, I was able to pick up another job for the semester, some more of the same kind of clerical work, also on campus, but I can work around my other job, so…weekends and evenings."

I could feel Jane's laser-like focus on me and I tried hard not to give any kind of tell that I was holding back something important. I ignored her, and kept my gaze on Lily.

"Well, that'll be nice for your checkbook, but are you sure that won't stretch you too thin? Two jobs, full load of classes?"

"And partying," Jane added, making Lily and me smile, for which I was grateful.

"No worries," I said and tweaked Jane's big toe through her sock. "I will have my priorities well in place. Partying first, for sure."

"Damn straight," she said. Lily just rolled her eyes at both of us and turned on to her back, staring up at the ceiling.

Eager to turn the conversation off of me and my new job— let alone my new boss—I said to Lily, "So, how did bringing Lucas home to meet the family go?"

A wide smile crossed her face first, and Jane poked me with her foot to make sure I'd noticed. I had. But then Lily's smile faded a bit and more of a melancholy look took over her beautiful face. "It went okay. No, I guess better than okay. Or at least better than I'd expected."

"Lots of covert sneaking into each other's rooms at night

after Mommy and Daddy went to bed?" Jane asked.

Lily took a deep breath, then let it out in a sigh. "Well, no, not really. And not for lack of trying on my part. Lucas got all weirded out about sleeping together in my parents' house. Said it would be disrespectful or something."

Jane hooted with laughter and Lily shot her a glare, but then softened and laughed along. "I know. Ridiculous, right? But I couldn't sway him. He came back to Schoolport on New Year's Day. I can't wait to see him." As if on cue, Lily's phone buzzed and she smiled as soon as she looked at the screen. She answered in a low voice and looked around the room. I motioned for her to take her love-talk call in my room and she nodded and got off her bed and left the room, closing the adjoining door behind her. Leaving Jane and me alone.

"So, how was your sister's wedding," I asked, even though we'd talked about it on the phone already. I kind of wondered if, now that time had passed, and we were together in person and not on the phone, she'd be more forthcoming about the guy she'd danced with. And kissed.

"Half sister," she clarified. "And like I said on the phone, it was fine."

I didn't want to push, because I certainly didn't want her pushing me for any details, but I couldn't stop myself. "So, no good guys there? With all of the groom's friends?"

She snorted. "Those guys couldn't get away from me soon enough. My…half brother, Joey, took me off the hands of the groomsman assigned to dance with me, and you've never seen a look more filled with relief."

I crossed my legs and turned to face her more fully. "Oh, come on, I'll bet you looked fantastic. You're telling me not one guy showed any interest?"

Another snort, but it took a longer time coming and didn't have quite the…oomph as the one previous. "Does an eighty-year-old geezer with wandering hands count? I told you about him, right?"

"Yes," I said, studying her carefully. Perhaps a bit *too* carefully, as she narrowed her eyes at me. "Why all the questions about guys at the wedding?"

Did I dare tip my hand? Mention I heard she had danced—and kissed—someone other than the old goat Senator? But that could all lead back to Montrose, and Jane was one sharp cookie.

I waved a hand nonchalantly, as if the question had minimal merit to me. "Just wondering if *anyone* got lucky over break. Sounds like Lily got frozen out by Lucas' good-guy morals."

"I kind of don't blame him, though," Jane said, surprising me. Jane was always one to rebel against what was expected of her. "I mean, Grayson Spaulding can be a formidable opponent. I think Lucas is smart enough to know that he should stay on Grayson's good side if he's going to go long term with Lily."

"You've been around them more than I have. Do you think that's the play? Long term?"

She looked thoughtful for a moment, then nodded her head. "Yeah, I do. They've got a lot going against them…but… yeah, I think so. I know *they* think so."

Wow. Halfway through freshman year and Lily was in deep. A third of our group was basically on the bench.

Jane and I looked at each other, neither one of us willing—or able—to talk about the men that may, or may not, be our equivalent of Lily's Lucas.

Lily came back into the room then, and it seemed irrelevant to ask her if she wanted to go out tonight, it was obvious by her smile she'd be seeing Lucas later.

We spent the next couple of hours before Lily left just sitting on the beds and shooting the shit.

Lily didn't stop talking about Lucas.
Jane didn't bring up Ponytail.
I never mentioned Montrose.

FOURTEEN

I WON'T BE IN *until after four.* I texted to Montrose Sunday morning. I'd received a call from the people at the admin building. They wanted to do some last minute testing before the new system went live at midnight and asked if I could come in. I initially said I couldn't, but they must have been desperate because they offered triple-time pay, which I couldn't pass up.

No problem. Except, I'll miss you by an hour. I need to leave by three. Montrose replied to my text. I was already at the admin building, in my little cubicle, going through the list of data that needed to be entered. It was a long list, and I'd be hard-pressed to make it to Snyder Hall by four, but I'd wanted to give Montrose some time to expect me.

My disappointment that I wouldn't see him at all threatened to pull me under. But then I remembered it was just the beginning of the semester, and we would have a lot of time together.

I knew I needed to be careful with Montrose and not let the intensity of my feelings show through or I was sure he'd be scared off. I also couldn't let him know that I'd basically been in love with him (at least from afar) for five years.

I definitely needed to follow his lead on this—showing only as much commitment and emotion as he did.

It was kind of like making sure I bought the right kind of

boots. I wanted to fit in to Montrose's life as much as I wanted to look like the Bribury girls.

So of course I didn't text back asking where he was going this afternoon. *That's too bad. But lots there to keep me busy.* I replied. Cool. Casual. All business. I had to physically put the phone down so I wouldn't keep texting.

I have to meet with the rest of the department to learn the new grading system. Though I suppose you could probably show me that.

I probably could. *I was tasked with ways of breaking the system, so probably not the best person to show you how to use it correctly.*

Is that what you're doing today? Breaking the system I'm taking the time to learn?

Kind of. I'll be careful not to take down anything you might need later.

Big of ya.

All for the greater good of my fellow Bribury students.

There was a pause, and I put my phone down again, thinking that if the conversation was over, I wasn't going to be the one typing over and over "Are you still there?"

Sorry. He finally typed. *You just reminded me you're a student. As if the faculty event last night wasn't reminder enough.*

I wanted to deflect and distract him from the fact that I was a student, but really, there was no deflecting it. It was a fact. Instead I texted *How was the event last night?*

Good, actually. Much as I would have liked to stay exactly where I was. Which was on his office couch, kissing the crap out of me. *I really enjoyed it. Of course, with that group, the subject of books we've read recently came up and so that was a good conversation.*

Anybody read the new John Irving and have anything to say? I finished it over break.

You worked two jobs AND had time to read Irving's latest? He's not exactly a quick read.

I TOLD you I could handle two jobs and classes.

Yeah, if you can handle Irving, what's a little Advanced Chem?

Haha.

Actually, yeah, I heard someone talking about the new Irving book. It wasn't in the group I was sitting with, though, so I didn't catch what they were saying.

Too bad. I'd like to hear someone in the literary world's thoughts on it.

What are YOUR thoughts on it?

He'd spent the evening amongst Bribury's strongest literary minds and wanted *my* opinion? Umm…no. I wasn't going to open myself up like that. I wasn't about to make him question my suitability for this job by trying to sum up a very complex author's newest masterpiece.

I probably should get back to work here. Systems to break, after all.

Sure. Of course. But one more thing about last night.

Yes?

There were a bunch of times when I thought to myself, "Syd should be here with me, she'd love this." And then I would remember that you couldn't be with me. Not as my plus one or anything. But…well…I thought about you.

That's nice. It was more than "nice" to me, but again, I wasn't going to show my cards this early into the hand.

Did you think about me?

So much for showing my cards. Before I could stop my fingers, I texted back. *I think about you all the time.*

A moment of inactivity. I willed the dots showing he was typing to start growing, but nothing.

Then, after what seemed like an eternity, a simple, *Me too.*

I foolishly hoped that Montrose had blown off his training session, or that maybe it had been cancelled and he'd still be in his office when I arrived around four-thirty, but no.

It was obvious he'd been there, though, and also obvious— at least to me—that he'd spent a fair amount of time going through the Esme/Rachel pile. The stack was still neat and tidy, but in a different order than I'd originally organized it.

I wondered if there was a reason he'd reordered the pieces of paper, and decided to work on a different stack tonight in case he wanted to clarify something with me first.

I took the pile I'd named *One Mile Trot* with me to the desk, where I saw a note he'd left for me on top of his laptop.

I won't need my laptop tonight, so if you'd rather work on it, go ahead. At the very least, transfer over the work that you've got transcribed to my machine when you're done. I might get a chance to go over it tomorrow before my first class.

I liked working on my machine, so I pushed his laptop to the side of the desk, pulled the *One Mile Trot* pile to just within reach and began typing.

After I finished transcribing the stack of papers, I spent a fair amount of time cutting and pasting and moving passages about to try and create some kind of cohesiveness to his various trains of thought. When I was pleased with the results, I transferred the files I'd created onto a flash drive that Montrose had left on top of his laptop.

Booting up his laptop, I packed mine away in my backpack. I was a little uncomfortable with poking around on his computer, but I supposed that many literary assistants had this kind of access to the machines of the authors they worked for.

And, he probably wouldn't have left all his downloaded porn, or sensitive love letters to past girlfriends, out on the desktop and then leave a note for me to use it.

Nope. No porn. On his fairly empty desktop was a folder titled "WIP" which I took for Work In Progress. Opening it, I found five more folders named by the past five years.

His notes had all been dated at the top, but I wasn't sure if the dates he scribbled the note necessarily coincided with the year from his folders. Probably not, as even with *Trot* there were notes from several different years.

I opened the most distant year's folder, from five years ago. In it were at least forty Word docs, all named with what looked to be different book titles. And also a corresponding file with the title and "notes." None of them were titles of the copious piles of notes I'd unpacked and sorted.

Perhaps the notes for these books were in the boxes still at his apartment?

I opened all the years' folders to find the same thing, only there were progressively more files in the ensuing years. I matched up the names with the piles of notes I had created. They were all accounted for, but there had to be at least an extra two hundred files. Were there *that* many boxes at Montrose's apartment?

Suddenly I was extremely grateful that I'd put so much time in during the holidays and got through all the boxes in his office. I was thinking I was over halfway done with the organizing part of this large project.

Now I realized I probably wasn't even close.

I opened the files for *Trot* and its notes, intending to see where it would make the most sense to add on the material from the flash drive.

The notes file was empty, but the book file started with the two words every voracious reader loved to see—Chapter One.

Yes, the character introduced on the first page matched the pile of notes I'd just transcribed, and I scrolled down to continue, resigning myself to a long evening ahead, spending time with my favorite author and his next—or possibly his next—book.

Except, there was nothing to page down to, nothing beyond the opening paragraph or two. Disappointed, I quickly realized that that's why I was here. So I could add notes and he'd be able to continue. Though, looking at it from solely a reader and transcriber's point of view, his notes were almost too random, too esoteric, to be called an outline or plot points, or anything close to a story structure.

Undeterred, I plugged in the flash drive and transferred my whole folder onto his desktop. I ejected the drive and put it in my bag to have as backup, then returned to his files.

I opened my *Trot* file from his desktop, copied all, then pasted it into his "*One Mile Trot* Notes" document. That way he'd have all the transcribed and organized notes in one place, my transferred folder, but also in the notes doc for each book title. I wasn't sure what I would do with the files I had that didn't match up with a title for which he'd already created a Word doc. I grabbed some scratch paper from my bag and jotted down the ones that didn't match, so I could ask Montrose about them later. I also wrote a note to him, describing the approach I took and that he could find my transcriptions in two spots on his computer.

Then I set about lots and lots of copy and paste.

It was the same for each document that I pasted my work into. The notes doc would be empty and the main doc would have two or three paragraphs of chapter one. No more. Not on one single document of the over forty I had transferred from the flash drive.

Curious, and basically done for now, I selected all of the main Word docs from every year and opened them all at once. The documents flying open on top of each other seemed to go on and on. My eye was not quite fast enough to see if any went beyond a few paragraphs, but it didn't look like it.

I started reading each of the docs—it didn't take long—and closing them when done. Just doing some quick math in my head, it seemed like he had enough different chapter ones of different stories to have started something new each week for the past five years. It probably wasn't exactly how it had happened, but that's what it would have averaged.

I had no idea how authors work, but I would have imagined that no matter how much tinkering with different ideas, at some point they committed and got to at least page two.

Billy Montrose had been literarily paralyzed for five years. No wonder he'd come to Bribury to shake things up.

I thought of our kisses yesterday. Yes, he was definitely shaking things up.

The key in the door made me look up, and also made heat rush through my body. He had come back after his training session.

"I was hoping you might still be here," he said with a smile when he entered the office. I watched his quiet, graceful movements as he took off his coat and hung it on the hook behind the door, which he then closed. And locked.

Turning to me, he saw how my gaze went from the locked door up to his face and he grinned. Right then I couldn't have told you one character name from the multitude I'd just read and typed.

The only name I could think of was Montrose. The only plot point I wanted to document was getting beneath him on the old leather couch in the corner.

The only character arc that seemed relevant was mine… and his.

Looking at me like that, his hair slightly wet from the snow outside, his grin both promising and devilish, I wanted to arc his brains out.

He crossed to me, and like he did yesterday, he penned me in with a hand on his desk and one on the back of my chair, which he turned to face him.

"I'm really glad you're here," he said, leaning in for a soft, barely-there kiss. My head followed him as he retreated, then fell back against the chair, as if a string had been cut.

I smiled up at him. "Me too. Do you want to go over what I got done? I left you notes on it, but—"

"Later," he said. He glanced at the desk, seeing his computer open. "As long as it's all on my machine I can look—" He did a double take at the screen, registering what files were open. "What...what are you doing?"

I briefly explained the whole process, but he wasn't listening. He pushed on the arm of my chair, wheeling me a little beyond the well of the desk, which he stepped into. His arms no longer penned me in, but instead were placed firmly on either side of his laptop as he began clicking through all the different chapter one documents, though, unlike me, he didn't take the time to read each one.

By the look of his face clouding over, something told me he didn't need to reread each one, he probably did so all the time.

And I also realized that maybe I'd screwed up.

FIFTEEN

·⟨⟩·

I AGAIN TRIED to explain what I'd done with the files, but it was like he couldn't hear my voice, he just kept clicking each document closed one by one, his eyes becoming that darker grey as he worked.

Finally, I edged him out of the way, and swiped the cursor across, catching all the files and closing them all at once.

He stayed where he was, leaning over, one hand still on the desk, the one I'd nudged now dangling lifeless by his side. His eyes stayed on the empty screen. I pointed to where I copied my folder of transcribed work and he silently nodded.

I sat back in my chair, willing myself not to speak, knowing that I probably wouldn't say the right thing. He was obviously embarrassed that I'd seen the fruit—or lack of—his labor for the past five years. That embarrassment now looked like it was turning into a healthy dose of anger. I learned from my stepfather that it was best in these situations to not speak first.

That, and become as small and invisible as you possibly could.

"I know I said you had free rein as far as giving feedback, and I did ask you to transfer your files to my machine, and we never really discussed boundaries...but...I..." He shook his head as he stood straight, running a hand over his chin and then placing both hands on his hips and turning toward the door.

Turning away from me.

A feeling of panic rose from me that I would lose this job, and whatever chance I had of being with—in whatever capacity—Montrose. And yet, I kept silent.

Like I said, I'd learned a lot from living with my stepfather.

"I mean," he continued, still not looking at me. "It's a weird situation. On one hand, as my assistant, *eventually* you would have had access to some of those files. Who knows, maybe all." I didn't miss the emphasis he put on "eventually." Clearly in his mind, we were not there yet on a working level. "But, in another aspect, you're someone I'm..." The hand across the chin again as he walked away from me, to the couch, where he sat, sinking down into the old, soft leather. He held his hands palm up, as if that would help him put a label on us. It didn't help and his hands dropped to his lap. "I don't know. Whatever *we* are. It's early, yes, but it feels like over the last three weeks and all our talks that we missed a few steps. Doesn't it? Like we were on the accelerated course?" He looked directly at me as he asked and I nodded, wheeling the chair back into place behind the desk, as if needing its protection.

And noticing he had used the past tense "were" when summing us up.

He waved his hands in the air, then let them rest on his thighs. Yesterday, my legs had been pressed up against those rock-hard thighs, rubbing against them as we'd tried to get closer to each other.

"Whatever we've got going, I would never allow my... person in my life to read any of my works in progress. I guess I should have explained that, but..." he trailed off, leaning back into the couch. His body read defeated. And pissed off.

I could keep quiet no more, even though my hard-earned lessons whispered to me to keep my mouth shut.

"Look, I get that you're embarrassed, but—"

"Embarrassed?" he said, sitting up, his hands braced on his knees as if he could pounce at any moment. "It's not about being embarrassed. I'm not *embarrassed* by my work. Any of it." There was a touch of defensiveness in his voice and also hubris, and I saw the first sign of the affected person he'd sworn he had been near to becoming. Yeah, not a real stretch to imagine him at full blown artistic prick.

"It's about feeling violated. Having someone go through my private work. Someone who I'm seeing. Yeah, violated. Like…"

At the word "violation" my throat got tight and I felt a tingling at the back of my neck. If he brought up an analogy like his house had been broken into, I'd let it slide. But anything else, anything more—

"Like I'd been ra—"

"Stop," I said, jumping out of my chair and holding my hand up. All thought of letting Billy Montrose lead in whatever dance we were doing flew out of my mind, and pure, raw emotion—most of it anger—fueled me as I pointed at him. "Do not say it. You have not been raped. You have not been violated in a physical way. Someone you're…seeing looked at your work, which you would have preferred to be private until you were ready to share."

He started to rise, but either the look on my face, or his own emotions, kept him on the couch.

"You are not harmed, you have not lost anything. You were not…violated." My voice was strong and pure and just a tad bit violent, but I didn't care. Later I was sure I would regret telling him off. I would tell myself that making this point wasn't worth losing Montrose—or a good-paying job—over. But right now…right now I knew I had to make my case.

I took a deep breath, signaling the end of my tirade, but I

didn't look away, didn't back down. I should have been scared shitless that I'd ruined everything. But honestly? It was the most...fearless I'd felt in five years.

His eyes narrowed at me and I realized that either he was going to come back at me hard, or worse, he was going to figure out something about me that I didn't want him to know.

That I didn't want anybody at Bribury to figure out. Something I wanted buried back in Queens and not to be a part of the new me.

I snatched my backpack from the floor, now thankful that I'd packed it earlier, and could just grab it, my coat, and go.

Montrose started to rise but I gave him a hand out to stop and he did, though he watched me as I took my coat from the coatrack, disentangling one of my sleeves from his.

"I like this job, and would like to keep it. But I understand if it's now too uncomfortable for you. If you'd like to get someone else, I'll understand. Just send me an email before tomorrow afternoon, so I won't come in."

"Syd," he said from behind me, but I had everything I needed now and just shook the back of my head at him and walked out the door.

I walked quickly down the hallway, sliding my coat on as I did. Half of me wanted him to follow me, to shout for me to stop. The other half dreaded the thought that he would.

I felt naked, like I'd become someone that I couldn't be, someone who would not fit into this world of the elite.

Someone I'd worked so hard to abandon.

I got to the main door of Snyder and walked outside. The snow was falling and I was glad because it blurred my vision as I turned to look at Montrose's office window.

But even through the falling flakes, and, okay, yes, maybe some falling tears, I saw the movement of the blinds as Montrose pulled them back. And then let them fall back into place.

SIXTEEN

The next day, I checked my email from my cubicle at the admin building when I finished up my shift.

Nothing from Montrose.

It was the second week of January and my long hours at the admin building were over, the new front end system working well, with only a couple of glitches. Everybody at work today was celebrating and backslapping and the consultants were getting ready to move on to their next assignment. I would return to just a couple of hours late in the afternoon a few days a week.

The guy who had asked me out for New Year's Eve stopped by my cubicle and said goodbye and I wished him luck at his next stop.

I decided to have a long dinner alone at the caf and get my studying done there before heading to Montrose's office.

Having only had one day of classes so far, there wasn't much to do, but I got the reading done, not wanting to fall behind. I had worked like a dog to get in here, there was no way I was going to get bounced for poor grades. Still, it was work, and though I did enjoy it, it didn't come as effortlessly to me as it did to Jane, who seemed never to crack a book and still got great grades for the first semester. (Though I'd had to ask her several times before she put forth that information.)

I checked my text and email on the walk over to Snyder from the caf, not wanting to walk in only to have Montrose say, "Didn't you get the message? Your ass is out of here."

Not that he'd say it like that. He was a writer, after all.

No message from him. To my relief (and maybe a bit of disappointment) his office window was dark, my strategy of stalling paying off. I knocked on his office door, just in case, before letting myself in.

I was loud as I unlocked the door, even coughing, in case Montrose was there but had decided to take a nap on the couch or something, thus turning out the lights.

Not that I thought that would be the case, but I didn't want to take the chance of surprising or waking him and giving him even more reason to be pissed off at me.

He wasn't there. I hung up my coat, knit hat and mittens, and slid off my boots, putting them in the corner to dry out while I worked.

As I rounded his desk, the first thing I noticed was a space where his laptop had been. After yesterday, I guess I shouldn't have been surprised. Instead, there were a handful of flash drives and a note.

Unpacking my laptop and phone and other stuff from my bag, I read the note from Montrose.

Syd,

Sorry about the misunderstanding yesterday. Perhaps the best way to go about the work is for you to transfer all your transcriptions and outlines to a flash drive and just leave it on the desk. I'll take it from there.

My last class is done at three daily, so I plan to take classwork home, and read it from my apartment each night, leaving the office open for you to work.

Billy

Well, at least we weren't back to "Ms. O'Brien." But there

wasn't one shred of anything personal in that note. I know, because I read it fourteen times analyzing it for something—anything—that would make me think we were back on track on a personal level.

Much as I wanted to find something, it was all business. And designed in such a way that he wouldn't have to see me.

And, obviously, I wouldn't have access to his chapter one docs anymore.

All forty gajillion of them.

I pulled the next pile from the credenza. *Skylark* would be a fast pile to transcribe. I even considered not doing the process I went through with the *One Mile Trot* pile of cutting and pasting into different outline ideas. But no, even if that wasn't part of the job, per se, it was an element that I enjoyed and was sure would help Montrose whenever he got around to writing fresh.

I snorted into the silent room as I wondered to myself if the man even knew how to type the words "Chapter Two."

My anger rose as I entered the notes from the various pieces of paper, napkins, and backs of envelopes, into a cohesive document on my laptop.

Yes, we hadn't discussed boundaries for me as it applied to his past work. Or *lack* of it, as the case seemed to be. But, if I had just been his assistant, if we hadn't spent all those hours FaceTiming and talking and texting and discussing everything under the sun, would he still have flown off the handle at the thought that I knew he was basically a crippled writer for the past five years, unable, or unwilling, to go beyond three paragraphs?

If we hadn't pressed our bodies into each other, clinging together with a shared wanting. If we hadn't kissed for hours on the couch, would I, as nothing more than a glorified typist, have been permitted to see those all-mighty beginnings of some two hundred different novels?

But then I thought about the lovely clinging. And the kissing. And I knew I wouldn't trade having had that for anything.

Even if I would never have it again.

My anger dissipated into sadness for what wouldn't be, but I kept typing, even though my eyes got a little glassy and at one point I couldn't even read my screen through the unshed tears.

Part of me even understood what made him lose it yesterday. (Not that he *really* lost it—I knew real losing it.)

The insecurity he felt as a writer, something I supposed every writer or artist went through at times, was something I very much understood.

His numerous chapter ones were the equivalent of my standing at the mall, staring at racks of shoes or clothing on a semi-regular basis because I'd noticed a new trend with the Bribury girls.

I knew insecurity. And I knew the feeling of shame at having your insecurities found out, like when those Bribury bitches called me a poser to Jane.

I shoved the *Skylark* pile a little further away from my keyboard, but still within reading distance. The tears were falling now. Not hard, and not often.

But there was no way I was going to leave my tearstains on Billy Montrose's papers.

SEVENTEEN

❖

I GOT INTO A ROUTINE. I would go to class, then spend two or three hours at the admin building, where the workload was light enough that I sometimes even got my studying done while there.

Afterward I would text Lily and Jane that I was going to the caf for dinner. Lily would meet me most nights, and we'd have dinner and then maybe study right at the caf or walk over to the library. Lucas worked nights, so Lily did most of her studying then, preferring to spend every moment that she didn't have class during the day with her man.

Jane was rarely available to join us for dinner. In fact, I didn't see much of Jane at all until late in the evenings. And by then, both of us were kind of burnt out and we had pretty surface conversations before calling it a night. Most nights when I came home from working in Montrose's office, Lily would be asleep and Jane would either be asleep or not there at all.

She got a new car, a gift from her father. Or bribe, she called it. I hadn't seen it yet, but she said it was a Corvette, which seemed kind of unlike Jane, but I guessed she didn't get to pick it out herself. Seemed like it would have been a better bribe if it was a kind she wanted, but maybe the surprise element of it was what her father was going for.

After I'd have dinner and a study session with Lily, I'd go to Montrose's office and get a few hours of work in, telling Lily I was off to my second job.

Each night he would leave a note—and more flash drives if needed—on what pile he'd like worked on next.

When I was done, I'd leave the flash drive in the middle of his desk blotter (never needing to move a laptop to make room, because he never left his again), with a note on how much I'd gotten done and where I'd left off.

When I was done with a complete pile, I'd do the cutting and pasting thing for it, then put all the notes and papers back in a box, labeled more clearly this time by the title of the book. Those completed boxes I put in the corner of his office with a paper over them that read "done." That area of boxes grew as the piles on the credenza decreased.

I wasn't exactly stalling and dragging this project out, but I didn't break my fingers by speed typing, either.

I knew there were still a lot more boxes at his apartment and once I was finished here we'd have to figure out how we wanted to attack those.

A part of me hoped that the longer I took with this batch, the higher the chance that Montrose might thaw, and when it was time to make the decision, he'd opt for me working out of his apartment.

That would force us to be in the same room at least, though I suppose he could probably just stay at the office crazy late.

I got paid by the job, not the hour, so I never felt guilty if I just stopped typing for a while, took small breaks, and, I don't know, stared at the photo of Montrose and his sister that sat on his desk.

His smile was broad and happiness was all over his face in the photo. He had smiled at me like that. While FaceTiming on New Year's Eve, when we'd joked about something. When he had walked into this office on his first day back and found me sitting at his desk.

Although that smile had quickly turned heated, and less of happiness and more of pure want. My want, my desire, for him did not decrease even though my only contact with him was through notes left on his desk.

Even though it had been several weeks, I could still feel his hands on my butt, still taste his kiss.

I knew I would never forget.

A few days before Valentine's Day (which fell on a Saturday this year), I received a text from a Bribury girl I'd partied with a little bit fall semester letting me know where the best party for guy hunting would be on Saturday night.

Samantha Martin was from old money, with a family pedigree that went back to the Mayflower. She was also the biggest partier I'd met at Bribury. She was the one Bribury Basic with whom I most wanted to cultivate a friendship. She always knew exactly what to wear, and which functions to attend.

I had texted her like crazy fall term, asking where she'd be on the weekend, stuff like that. She'd always been friendly when I'd seen her, but I suspected that she might have been the one to originally put the label of poser on me that Jane so effusively shot down.

I supposed normal girls did this sort of thing all through high school, but I was just trying to stay alive and invisible during my high school years, and missed out on all the joys of frenemy bullshit.

It was immensely satisfying that she was the one texting me this time with party deets. And also satisfying that I hadn't even once thought to text her yet this semester.

Personal growth, or Montrose obsession?

Probably a little of both.

I knew it was a given that Lily would be with Lucas on Saturday but since Jane hadn't mentioned the ponytail guy at all, I asked her if she wanted to go out with me that night to the party Samantha had suggested.

She didn't seem too excited about it at first, and I was ready to let it drop, but midweek she said yes.

I had a sense of dread about the whole upcoming weekend. If things weren't going to happen with Montrose, it was time for me to move on, and see what might happen with a Bribury guy. I had checked out a few in the fall. Some had blown me off, some had shown some interest.

And yet, my heart wasn't in it. The Bribury guys that I'd noticed, or hooked up with, didn't appeal to me anymore.

I only wanted Montrose.

That option apparently not on the table, I tried to garner up the enthusiasm to go through with the evening that I'd cajoled Jane into.

I went to my closet and picked out the tightest red dress I owned and put it aside to wear on Saturday, talking Jane into doing the same. She ended up borrowing one from Lily. I didn't think Jane owned any man-hunting clothes.

Weekends were weird, with Montrose and me carefully planning when we'd each be at his office so we wouldn't have to spend much—if any—time together. It was like divorced parents divvying up custody of the kids—I had the office in the mornings, he had it in the afternoons.

That morning the campus was deserted, students sleeping in from their Friday night reveling. Fresh snow had fallen in the night and crunched beneath my shoes as I tromped to Snyder.

The office was exactly how I'd left it last night when I'd finished up at eight. I knew I would most likely be the next person in, but I'd left a note for Montrose with where I'd left off, just in case he'd...what? Decide to make a late night visit to his office to see my handwritten note? To marvel at my stellar typing?

Yeah, maybe I was just hoping he had nothing better to do on a Friday night.

I had come to terms—sort of—with the idea that I'd blown it with Montrose. (Even though I wasn't sorry in the least for speaking up that day.) That whatever we'd had, whatever flirting we'd done online, and the day of kissing, was all there was going to be.

But I hadn't let my mind wander beyond that. If Montrose wasn't texting, FaceTiming, or kissing me…was he doing all of that with someone else?

Thinking about it should have made me mad, or certainly sad, but instead, I felt that old familiar insecurity wash over me. Like I'd shown up at a Bribury party in last year's jeans or something.

I hated that feeling. Absolutely hated it. I knew I had a chip on my shoulder about it, the size of Queens itself, but I didn't seem to have the tools to get past it.

Not yet, anyway.

I tried to shake off my feelings, and not think about where Montrose had spent his Friday night. Or with whom.

A stack of papers from the class he taught had been placed on the now nearly-empty credenza. I'd ignored it yesterday, but today I thumbed through them, remembering turning in this assignment myself last fall.

Had another student's papers captured Montrose's attention, like he purported mine had? After skimming a few of them, I picked up the last pile of book notes from the other end and got to work.

I was done about two hours later, and put the notes in a box, labeled it by book title and stacked it on top of the others in the corner.

I spent another hour working on the notes I'd transcribed, then transferred the file to a fresh flash drive and placed it in the center of the blotter. I didn't bother leaving a note, it was obvious where I'd left off.

I packed up my laptop, and pulled my coat off the hook. I took my shoes back to the desk to sit while I laced them up.

As I slid into my shoes, my eyes were drawn to the photos on Montrose's desk as they so often were.

I wanted this job. I needed the money, and I loved being just a little inside the mind of Montrose. But it was hard being here, seeing his smiling face as I worked. Knowing that old leather couch had been the site of the best kisses I'd ever tasted.

I grabbed a sheet of paper from the side of his desk and scribbled a note, saying some—but not all—of what I was feeling, before I could think better of it.

Billy,

As you can see, all the materials that were in the office have been completed. The last of it is on the drive on your desk. This might be a good time for me to break away from the project. You've paid me for January and February, already, so we could call it even.

If you'd like to have someone else finish up the job, I'll completely understand.

If I don't hear from you by Monday at four, I won't plan on coming in and will consider our professional relationship fulfilled.

I didn't apologize for going after him about the whole rape/violation tantrum. And I added in "professional" when describing our relationship, though it probably wasn't necessary.

Professional was the only type of relationship we had.

I half hoped when he came in on Monday morning that he'd text me right away and tell me to plan on working, that he'd brought a couple of boxes from his apartment and I could begin with phase II. My other half, my less masochistic side, wanted to receive no such text. To be done with the torture of being so close to him, and yet so, so far away.

Before I could grab the note and tear it up, I quickly left the office.

EIGHTEEN

⋆⁖⋆

I GRABBED SOME LUNCH by myself at the caf and decided to get in a few hours at the library before I needed to get back to my room and start getting ready for the night out with Jane.

Around three, I got a text. Because I had my phone on silent, it was just sheer luck that I saw the light go on out of the corner of my eye. Probably Jane, wondering when we should be ready to go out.

I started to pack my bag as I swiped my phone. It was like my hand holding my laptop hovered in the air and froze when I realized that it was Montrose, not Jane, who had texted.

First text in over a month from him. It had all been short notes on his desk since that Sunday night before classes started.

Are you on campus?

I set my laptop down, and took a deep breath before answering yes, and that I was in the library.

Can you come back to the office for a little while?

I didn't hesitate. *Yes. I'll be there in about ten minutes. Are you there now?*

Yes. See you soon.

I threw my stuff in my bag and made my way quickly through the stacks and out of the library.

He hadn't mentioned why he wanted me to come, nor for how long he thought we'd be there. But, he'd obviously seen my note. So, either he wanted to fire me face-to-face, or he was going to tell me that I was still on the job.

But why not say that with a simple text or email?

It would be the classy thing to do to let me go in person. Realizing that was probably the reason for the summons, my footsteps slowed. Crap. The last thing I'd want to do after being dumped (again!) by Montrose was to go out and party with Jane in our slutty red dresses.

I could just see myself getting drunk and being the girl who spends the night crying into her beer, telling her sad tale of woe to anybody who would listen.

Which of course I could never be. My tale of woe with Montrose could not be made public.

I texted Jane and told her I was sorry, but I had to work tonight, and to go without me. She responded quickly that it was no big deal, and she was cool with staying in.

Again I wondered about the ponytail guy from Betsy Stratton's wedding, and if he was the reason Jane seemed to be a bit mellower this semester.

And had no plans for Valentine's Day.

I debated quickly running back to Creyts to change my clothes or at least put on some makeup. Knowing there wouldn't be a chance of running into Montrose during my "visitation" hours of the office, I'd just thrown on some Lulus, a knit top and sweater this morning. I'd twisted my hair up in a messy bun and left, figuring I'd shower later, before getting ready for the party.

But if there was a slight chance of Montrose getting tired of waiting for me and leaving, then I would risk showing up as I was.

Dusk was falling now, and as I approached Snyder Hall I could see the lights on from Montrose's window, though the blinds were closed.

I knocked on his office door instead of using my key. To hear his voice tell me to come in sent a chill through me. I had missed that deep, husky voice.

"Hey," he said as I entered and closed the door behind me. "Thanks for coming on such short notice. Especially since you've already been here today. Take off your coat, have a seat."

I nodded as I moved into the office, noticing several new boxes on the credenza, which had been empty when I'd left a few hours ago. I took my coat and hat off and hung them on the hook next to his long coat. "No problem," I said. I motioned to the new boxes. "Are these the ones from your apartment?"

He nodded, not rising from his seat. "Some of them. There are still a few left, but...you can get to those last."

I raised a brow at his use of me in the future tense, at least as it pertained to the job.

"I don't want you to leave the job, Syd. You've done a great job so far." He looked down at the top of his desk, then back up at me, the dim light from his desk lamp reflected off his grey eyes. "Unless, you'd *rather* leave?" He tried to keep his voice level and indifferent, but I heard it. That tiny tone of questioning, of...insecurity.

"I'd like to stay on. I'm really enjoying the work."

He visibly relaxed, sitting back in his chair. I felt a huge sense of relief myself, and sat down in the guest chair in front of his desk. Normally, I wouldn't like the dynamic of the seating, like I was being interviewed or a student of his or something. But the truth was, that's all I was, his employee, waiting for further direction.

Yes, this was the seat for me. Not on the couch with him by my side. Not sitting on the edge of his desk in front of him. And certainly not sitting on his lap.

Still, it felt oddly...formal.

I looked across the desk at him. He was wearing a Brown

University hoodie and jeans. His hair looked like he'd been running his hands through it, his regular stubble had at least another day on it, and I suspected that I wasn't the only one who had skipped the shower this morning.

But God, to see him again, when I'd been just basically staring at his picture for the last month. To me, he was perfection.

"Good, I'm glad," he said about my wanting to stay on the job.

"Besides," I said, "now that we have this system worked out, it's been going really smoothly." I tried to keep my voice light, like it wasn't a huge blowup and the demise of whatever personal interaction we'd begun that caused us to come to this new working arrangement.

"Yeah, about that," he said. He leaned forward, placing his elbows on the desk and lacing his fingers together, like he was a doctor about to deliver terminal test results to his patient. "We need to talk about that night."

I braced myself. There was no way I was going to apologize for berating him for almost using the term rape. But… "I *am* sorry for what you felt was an intrusion on your privacy by reading your documents. It seemed to make sense to put the transcribed notes in the correct document, but I shouldn't have read all the chapter one documents." It was true I shouldn't have gone into all those documents. It was clear that my files could have been left on their own, or at the very least, put in the "Notes" doc for each book. I didn't need to read them all. Although, a heads-up from him about not wanting to share those docs would have helped the whole situation.

(Yeah, I might have still looked, not sure about that.)

"I could have been more clear about where to put everything on my computer," he easily conceded. He ran a hand over his chin, then leaned back in the chair and looked to a point just beyond me. A look I knew well from his class.

He let out a deep sigh. "I've even been wondering if it wasn't some kind of Freudian slip on my part? If maybe I purposely didn't give you more specific instructions?" His gaze came back to me. "If maybe I actually *wanted* you to read my stuff?"

"Maybe," I said, not immune to fucked-up logic, having had a lifetime of it myself. "But then why the freak out? And to such an intense level?"

"I'm really sorry about that. About using that verbiage." He sat forward again, as if physically, as well as verbally, pleading his case. "You were right. It's not a word to be used in any sense except literally. And I don't mean "literally" as it's being used today."

"You mean figuratively?" I said, daring to crack a bit of a smile.

"God, don't even get me started on that whole thing." He waved a hand, his smile tentative, matching mine. "The bottom line is, I'm a writer. I, better than most people, know the power of words. And should also know when hyperbole is not only not needed, but downright offensive."

He searched my eyes, and I could sense he wanted me to pipe in, to tell him why I, personally, found his usage offensive. But I didn't say anything. Nor would I. Ever.

"I'm sorry," he finally said.

"Me too," I said, meaning that the whole damn thing had ever happened.

He nodded, seeming to bring that discussion to a close. Doing what looked like a mental head slap, he rose from his seat and moved to the credenza. "Oh, man, I don't want to forget this. Again."

I watched as he reached behind one of the boxes filled with his notes (and my next round of gainful employment!), and pulled out a wide, but fairly flat, gift-wrapped box with a bow on it.

He came around to my side of the desk and leaned against the front, facing me, offering me the box. "This is for you."

"It is?" I said, looking at the box like it might be a trap of some sort. We'd just come to an alliance about my continued working for him. Then to throw a gift into things? On Valentine's Day? "What is it?" I asked, still not reaching for it.

He leaned forward and placed the box on my lap. I almost opened my knees and shut them, catching his hand, like it was the *Pretty Woman* pearls. Oh, to have his hand between my legs.

But I was neither quick nor brave enough to pull it off, and he placed the box without touching me at all.

"Open it," he answered, giving me no clue as to its contents.

"But, why?" I asked, then began unwrapping it, sticking the bow to the arm of my chair.

"I got it for you in Gstaad. I'd intended on giving it to you that first day I got back, I even had it in my bag. But I got... distracted."

I looked up at him and raised a brow, knowing full well what had distracted him. My mouth. My body. My kisses.

He cleared his throat before continuing, but I did notice his gaze had dropped to my mouth. "Anyway. Instead of a holiday gift, I guess it has become a peace offering of sorts."

"But...today?"

"Why not today?" he asked.

I looked at him questioningly, but he just shrugged, not knowing what I was getting at. Sighing, I said, "Because it's Valentine's Day?"

The look on his face was classic Absent-Minded Professor. His gaze swung to the large wall calendar pinned up above the couch. "Aw, shit," he said as he acknowledged the date.

I lowered my gaze and continued to slowly unwrap the box, the thrill somewhat tarnished knowing that he hadn't meant anything romantic by his gift-giving timing. My hands were sure, though my emotions weren't, as I slid the wrapping paper from the box, which had some French name on the cover embossed in gold.

He sighed, though I didn't look up. I heard him whisper, "Fuck it," under his breath, not sure if I was supposed to hear it or not. Suddenly he was on his haunches in front of me, his hands stilling mine, sliding under them, so that our palms met.

I stared at our joined hands, until he laced his fingers with my willing ones, then I looked up into his grey gaze. His eyes weren't the stormy seas, but that of a crisp, cold winter sky.

"Syd, will you be my Valentine?" he whispered.

I gave one tiny nod, which he noticed and let out a held breath. Good, he was as nervous as I was. And double good, he wanted to get back on track to...wherever we had been headed.

"Of course, it depends," I added.

He looked concerned, but I must have had some kind of teasing tell, because he got a grin on his face, quirked one brow and said, "On what?"

"On what's in the box," I said, then smiled at him. A wide, sincere, and oh, so inviting smile.

"Sorry to say, it's not *that* kind of gift. But you have definitely given me some ideas for next time."

I didn't comment that there wouldn't be a next time. Or at least not a next Valentine's Day. He would be back in New York next year, his year of teaching—and getting his writing mojo back—over.

Whatever we were venturing into, whatever we were stepping up to, would be over in May when the semester was.

Did anybody, ever, lament the end of school as I did?

"Though it *is* something you can wear," he added. "Just...

above your clothes, not underneath them.

I had the cover off and slid back the tissue paper to find a beautiful, multi-colored scarf.

It wasn't like any of the ones I'd seen on the Bribury campus before. And certainly not in Queens. I removed it from the box and spread it open. It was larger than it first appeared, and so incredibly soft that I put it to my cheek. "It's beautiful," I truthfully said, even while I was wondering if I should wear it on campus. It was so different. But different in a good way, or different in a "look at that idiot" way?

"I know this isn't the type you, or your fellow students, are wearing, but I saw it and thought of you."

I held up the exquisite, and undoubtedly crazy expensive, piece of material. "This made you think of me?"

He shrugged, then settled his hands on the outside of my knees, his long fingers pointing up my thighs. "Yeah. It's kind of mainstream, because everyone's wearing scarves. And yet, it's really different, and isn't one everybody has. It's unique." I watched him as he spoke, his eyes locked on mine. "Even if it doesn't want to be."

He knew me well. Maybe too well. And yet, here we were, apologies made, seemingly picking back up with the personal end of things as well as professional.

"Yes, Billy," I said, not breaking eye contact. "I will be your Valentine."

He flashed the wide smile that he sported in the picture of him and his sister skiing. The one I'd stared at so many times while in this room.

He leaned forward at the same time I did and we met just over my knees for a sweet, feather-light kiss. His hands tightened on my thighs, more for balance than seduction, but I loved any time his hands were on me, for whatever reason.

It had been a long five weeks since he'd kissed me, and

this kiss he was giving me now, while sweet, and so well worth waiting for, wasn't enough. Wasn't nearly enough.

He opened his eyes and looked at me with those amazing grey orbs. As he pulled back, I could tell he was waiting for me to set the pace, to give the word that it was okay to go on.

And maybe I should have just thanked him for the scarf and then left. We probably shouldn't start something that, at best, would be frowned upon by the administration, and at worst could have him losing his position and me losing my scholarship.

But we'd thought that all out before and decided that the reward was definitely worth the risk. The time spent apart should have made me come to my senses about it all, but it had only made me miss what might have been even more. Made me more desperate to play out our hands. And mouths. And God, that awesome ass of his.

"I didn't lock the door when I came in," I said, lobbing the ball back to his side of the court.

"That's an easy fix," he replied, but there was a question in his voice. And he didn't move. He was hitting it back to me, barely getting the weak shot over the net.

"Billy?" I said, rushing the net for the smash.

"Yes?"

"Lock the door."

He was on his feet and heading to the door at record speed.

NINETEEN

⬧⬧⬧

WHEN HE RETURNED to stand in front of me he held a hand out and I took it, rising from my chair.

"I'm going to kiss you now," he said softly. Even though he'd just given me a sweet kiss, I knew this was different.

My breath hitched, but I tried not to show any other signs of my extreme anticipation. "Okay," I coolly said. I may even have shrugged a tiny bit.

His mouth—and those lips—quirked up in a little grin. "No. Really," he said, his face moving closer to mine.

"Okay," I repeated, with a little more emphasis.

"Like, I'm going to kiss the shit out of you."

I tilted my head a tiny bit to the side, and with a Queens girl toughness said, "Bring it."

He did.

Gone was the sweet softness from just a moment ago. Now, he took my face in his hands and brought his mouth down to mine, hard, determined. It was like the past month had never existed and I was back in his arms, tasting him, wrapping my arms around his neck, trying to get closer to his body.

"God," one of us groaned. I wasn't even sure which one. My breath seemed to leave my body and I gasped for air just long enough to return to his mouth.

His arms came around me, his hands sliding my sweater

up so he had access to my leggings-clad butt. Pulling me hard against him, he let out a little growl and squeezed.

"Billy," I moaned, digging my hands into his soft hair, grinding myself against him. It felt like a fever had finally broken. For me, a five-year fever. And I was still burning up. Burning for him.

"Christ, Syd," he hissed as I nipped his gorgeous bottom lip. "I knew we'd be...I just knew."

"Me too," I said, tipping my head back for him as he kissed under my jaw, licking and nibbling some wonderfully sensitive spots. He pulled my sweater up and I reluctantly separated my body from his and put my arms up to hasten the process of getting naked. I yanked at his hoodie and he helped, both garments tossed to the chair behind me. He was in a T-shirt and I had a long-sleeved shirt on, which were both pulled off with the same zeal.

Having dressed this morning with no idea where this day would end, I was happy to see I'd put on a decent bra.

Irrelevant, because it was on the floor in seconds, as were the rest of my clothes and his. Jeans and leggings and socks and shoes, all hurriedly taken from each other's bodies and discarded until he was down to his black boxer-briefs and I was only in my red panties.

"The lights," I said.

He shook his head. "No. I've waited so long to see you, there's no way I'm going to turn them off now."

"But you can see shadows from outside with the overhead light on. At least turn that one out."

He didn't ask how I knew that particular piece of information, just nodded and walked over to the switch by the door. Before he flipped the lights he looked back at me.

"Christ, you're beautiful, Syd."

I leaned back into the edge of the desk, placing my hands

down on both sides, near my hips, arching my back a tiny bit.

Even from the distance of the small room, I could hear him swallow.

"Turn on the desk lamp," he said.

I stretched behind me, never taking my eyes from his, and clicked on the lamp. It was one of those kinds with the soft, green shade and produced a soft, almost eerie glow that now backlit my body.

Billy's hand left the switch, with the overhead lights still on, and he placed his palm over his chest. "I have no words," he whispered.

I spread my legs a little bit more, wondering if my wetness was visible on my red cotton panties. I couldn't take my eyes off Billy to check.

He slid his hand down his chest, which was mostly smooth, with a smattering of hair at the top, and then a darkening line that he was now skimming to place his hand over his erection. He stroked himself over his briefs while I watched. When I brought my legs together to get a little relief, a wide grin spread across his face and he started to me.

"The lights," I said.

He laughed at his forgetfulness (fully understandable given the situation), hit the lights and came over to me.

I started to reach for him, but he just shook his head. "No, stay right there. Just like that." I did.

He bypassed me, though his eyes stayed on me, and went to the tiny closet in the corner where he pulled out a plaid blanket, which he unfurled on the couch, creating a covering sheet of sorts.

I raised a brow and he shrugged. "That leather sticks to your skin like a sonofabitch."

"You've done this a lot?"

He chuckled. "I take naps on here. Or did fall semester.

But, to answer your question, no. No, this couch has never seen as much skin as it's about to."

I smiled softly, my insecurity quelled.

He walked past me, nodding with his head for me to still stay at the edge of the desk. Going to his side of the desk, I watched over my shoulder as he took his keys from the blotter and unlocked one of the bottom desk drawers. From my angle, I couldn't see what was in it, but when he straightened, he had a box of condoms in his hand which he tossed on the couch as he—finally—made his way back around to me.

I nodded at the condoms. "Those been in there all year?"

He shook his head as his eyes roamed my body. "No. I brought them my first day back from break." He reached out and ran a cool finger along my clavicle.

So, they'd been in his bag the day we'd kissed for hours. I'd briefly wondered at the time if he hadn't gone further because of lack of protection.

As if reading my mind, or trying to put it at ease, he said, "I never took for granted that this would happen, Syd. I wanted to be safe if it did. But...this is still your call."

I took my hands from the desk and stepped away from it, and into him, wrapping my arms around his neck, pressing my naked breasts against his warm, strong chest.

"I want this, Billy. I've wanted this from the first."

"Me too," he whispered, ducking his head and kissing my neck as his hands splayed over my back, pulling me even closer still.

I didn't mention that my "from the first" started many years ago.

Sliding a hand under each of my thighs, he lifted me up and carried me to the couch where he sat first, then lowered me onto his lap. Face to face, my legs straddling him. I put my hands out to steady myself on the back of the couch behind his head.

The softness (or oldness) of the couch, and the weight of the two of us, made us sink in and so I was quite a bit higher than him. Which was perfect, because that put my breasts right at his eye level. And though I could stare into his gorgeous grey eyes forever, it was mind-blowing when he leaned forward and caught my nipple with his mouth.

I squirmed on him as I moaned in delight at his hands skimming up my sides and playing with my breasts, molding them, pushing them together, squeezing as he sucked on one, and then the other.

I kept one hand on the couch, and the other sank into his soft hair, playing with the strands, yanking a little as he bit down on my nipple.

"Christ," he groaned, but quickly returned to me, his mouth suckling with determination.

My hips started bucking into his, needing relief. The cotton of our underwear the only barrier between us.

"I know," he whispered. "I can't wait either." There was almost apology in his voice.

"Long enough," I gasped as I rubbed my clit down on his hard-on. "Waited long enough."

In one smooth movement, he twisted me and brought me down to the couch on my back while also peeling my panties off.

Finally, my fantasies were coming to life as he lowered himself down to me, my legs open and ready for him. I moved my hands down his back, rigid and rippled with strength, and slid his briefs down, then hung on to the ass I'd admired so often, as he quickly put on the condom and guided himself inside me.

I wanted to hang on to his body, to explore every inch with my fingers as he began a slow rhythm of gliding inside me, but instead I took his face in my hands as he looked down at me.

His strong musty scent mingled with the vague smell of closet from the blanket beneath me. I fought it back when I felt my eyes glistening with tears of happiness. I had loved this man for five years in a childlike way of worship and awe. And now, to have him moving inside me, staring down at me with such passion and desire in his eyes…

"Shhh, it's okay," he said, as if he sensed my imminent undoing. "We've got this. We'll do this together."

I nodded, not really knowing what he was saying, but not caring either. My mind couldn't think, couldn't grasp on to any thought as he began moving faster, the building friction both delicious and torturous.

He never took his eyes from mine and there was no way I could look away, nor did I want to.

His hand eased off my hip and slid around so he could play in my folds, tease me into even more.

"Together," he whispered, and I dumbly nodded. My body was his, and he could demand anything from it, even the timing of when I would come.

"Soon," he said, as my breath hitched. "Wait," he whispered as my muscles started tightening around him.

"Now," he groaned as my body exploded.

I held his biceps tight as I spasmed around him as he came. Never once taking my eyes from him, even to close them in satisfaction.

He kept on, and I gasped as ripple after ripple coursed through me. I ran my hands from his arms, down his sweat-glistened back to his ass, where I squeezed as he rocked into me, slowing…slowing.

Until finally our movements had stopped and the gasping for breath was the only sound in the tiny office.

He placed a soft kiss on my chest, right on my necklace from Jane.

"Happy Valentine's Day," I heard him whisper as I drifted off, still being held close to his chest.

TWENTRY

Montrose

I was lost in self-pity and doubt for five years.
And then she found me.

SYD O'BRIEN SLEPT IN MY ARMS, our limbs intertwined. She was nearly on top of me on the narrow couch. One of my hands was buried in that thick, soft glossy black mass of her hair, now completely out of its bun. My other hand rested on her smooth hip, holding her so she wouldn't slide off to the floor.

We would get to the floor eventually. We weren't nearly done with the couch.

And I *definitely* had plans for the scarf I'd given her.

It felt really odd to be with her. My growing feelings for her had very much been in my head these past seven weeks, due to being away from her. Though I found her incredibly attractive (okay, totally smokin' hot), and was attracted *to* her (okay, I had pretty much been sporting wood for the past seven weeks), all that FaceTiming and texting, had kind of become the norm.

Until my first day back when I had, indeed, kissed the shit out of her.

And then…nothing. For a month. A very, *very* long month. And all because I was an insecure, arrogant prick.

Diandra had called me that when we broke up. I thought, at that time, that she was just being bitchy about the break up, even though it had been her idea. But I realized soon after, that she was pretty much spot on.

Well, maybe not *soon* after. It took a couple of years for me to figure it out, and a few months after that to put in motion a plan to turn the slippery slope of prickness uphill.

Thus, my year at Bribury. I probably could have scored a guest lecture spot at one of the Ivy League schools, certainly at Brown, my alma mater. But, being a one-time deal, and a very big experiment, I went for a lesser known, but still considered high-brow college to teach at. And to try and get my head out of my ass.

So far? Well, I'd been too busy reading college freshmen papers to wallow in my lack of productivity.

I was also telling myself that said papers were the reason I hadn't gotten any real writing done.

Different day, same bullshit.

No, not the same bullshit. Syd O'Brien was lying in my arms after a most…thrilling evening. Shit, I was a writer and all I could come up with to describe the past two hours was thrilling? Yeah, maybe I was a totally overrated hack who caught lightning in a bottle once, never to repeat the experience.

Shit. Okay, I could do this. Making love with Syd had been…transcendental.

Christ. Transcendental?

As I often did, in my mind I saw my harshest critics' faces frowning at me. This time even Michiko Kakutani for the *Times*, who had loved *Folly*, was shaking her finger at me.

Yeah, so scrap transcendental.

Her skin was so smooth, her hair so silky…God, it was

all crap. All true, of course, but yeah, National Book Award winner Billy Montrose could not put the words together to describe the life-altering event of having sex with a girl.

But, it wasn't just any girl. It was Syd.

And, maybe life-altering was the best, or at least the most accurate, description to use, if not the most lyrical.

I'd noticed her in my class right away, of course, as the more interesting looking girl who always sat between the other two. One being Jane Winters who certainly made her intentions known right away, and Lily Spaulding who was breathtakingly beautiful.

I'd been given the codes of conduct when I started, and of course any kind of relationship with a student was verboten. And I had kind of scoffed at it. I hadn't dated a girl that young in…well, since I'd *been* that age. After Diandra, I had a couple semi-girlfriends, and they'd both been a few years older. A co-ed hook up was the last thing on my mind when I took the gig.

This year was supposed to be about finding my joy of writing again, by teaching it. And finally getting on track with my next book, whichever one that turned out to be.

Until I read Syd's first paper. The assignment for each freshman was a thousand words on how Bribury was different than what they had expected.

And the words flowed from her with purpose and strength. I could tell she'd probably whipped the thing off in a couple of hours, and yet it was the freshest, most insightful paper I read out of over a hundred students. As was her next one, and the next. And I found myself searching her out each time I entered the room.

Yes, Lily was beautiful, and Jane had this "it" thing going on that was appealing (and at times very annoying), but Syd, while quiet during class, and clearly embarrassed of Jane's antics, was the one with the still waters running deep essence about her.

And that essence was confirmed with each paper I assigned. I'm not really proud of it, but I did tweak some of the themes of the papers to feed Syd some of the things that I was curious about.

I told myself that it was good for all students to stretch themselves a little bit in their writing—and it was true. But, at some point, I started searching through the pile of turned-in papers to read hers first.

And last. I always read it last to give comments and a grade. But I read it first…just for me, I supposed.

I spent equal time on each student's paper with comments and feedback. Perhaps more time on the others' because with Syd's papers the comments flowed almost as effortlessly as her writing seemed to.

I knew of her guilt at leaving her little brothers behind in Queens. But also of the near desperateness in her to become something more than what she saw every day. There was obviously much more to the family dynamic at home than she disclosed in her writing. I could almost see the point where she would yank her fingers off the keyboard, teetering at the edge of the abyss of her deepest feelings. Then slowly edge herself back to safety.

That safety in her writing was something I wanted, as her instructor, for her to break through.

And as someone interested in her in other ways, I wanted to protect her from going beyond her safety point.

Coming out of your comfort zone was one thing. But I sensed with Syd there was something pretty deep that needed, at least for now, to continue hibernating.

Demons could be fought later on, when you were a bit more removed from them, and not when you were in a new environment, trying (in Syd's case, desperately) to fly under the radar and blend in.

She turned away from me and I took my hand out of her hair, watching the strands, so black against my winter-white hand, softly fall and drift down to lay against her back.

Her back to my chest, I considered waking her, but I let her sleep on. We'd gone at it hard, and for a long time. And though I had dozed for a little bit after, I was now too energized to snuggle into her without being selfish and rolling her under me for Round Two.

Or Four. Whatever, I'd stopped counting. (Who am I kidding, I'm a guy, we don't ever stop counting that kind of shit.) It would be Round Four.

Instead, I carefully extricated myself from behind her and swung one leg over those gorgeous, latte-colored thighs, and got up from the couch.

I grabbed my jeans from the floor and slipped them on, leaving the top button undone. (Chicks loved that, right?)

I took my long coat and covered Syd with it. It didn't quite reach her shoulders, and although I would have loved to see the creamy curves on display, I used the scarf I'd given her to place upon any exposed skin.

It was February after all. And the sweat we'd worked up (*a lot*) was cooling off now, at least on me.

I pulled my T-shirt from the floor, my hoodie from the chair, and put them on as I made my way around to my desk. I angled my chair so I could see both my laptop screen and Syd as she slept on.

Defenseless, her guard down, she seemed so much... softer. Watching her, I felt a small pang in my chest. I had better be careful here. Yes, Syd was from Queens, and one tough chick, but she was also young and I was in no position to offer anything more than this, what we'd just spent the last few hours engaged in.

For one, there was the student thing. I didn't think anyone would string me up for sleeping with my assistant after she'd been my student, only because I'd be gone in a few more months. It wouldn't be worth it to the administration.

And I didn't intend on continuing on with teaching, though I was enjoying it much more than I'd thought I would.

But it could hurt Syd. And that couldn't happen. Not because of me.

For another, I had no intention of starting *anything* long term. Not when I was trying—clawing—to get back to serious writing.

No. Not serious writing. I'd done plenty of that in the past five years.

I needed to do some serious *finishing*.

That's why it was so perfect for Syd and me—beyond the whole code of ethics thing. (I never had been one for codes being impressed upon me.) She knew I'd be gone in a few months, never to return. She had three more years here at Bribury in which to find something more serious—if that's even what she wanted.

The other reason it was perfect was although Syd was certainly a reader, she wasn't one of the many—*many*—women I'd encountered who wanted to "heal" me because they were obsessed with Aidan Colly of *Gangster's Folly* and mistakenly thought we were one and the same.

Yes, Syd was that great blend of someone I could hold a great conversation about books with, but who wasn't an overzealous Billy Montrose fan.

Though, shit, after making her come four times, she'd *better* be a Billy Montrose fan now!

Smiling at my own guy-ness, I started going through the notes she'd transcribed this morning.

God, had it just been this morning when she'd been here

and left the note about quitting?

A shot of panic swiped through me now as it had when I first read the note and realized that being an insecure ass was going to cost me something great.

I'd quickly gone back to my apartment, loaded up some more boxes to show her how much more I needed her. I had seen the gift-wrapped scarf on my coffee table where I'd thrown it the night that I'd thrown my little tantrum, and grabbed it too. I'd rushed back to the office, then texted her, holding my breath that she'd answer.

Yeah, there were a lot of moments in the past five years that I'd acted in a way in which I was embarrassed. But none more so than when I'd laid into Syd for reading my stuff.

And she'd nailed it at the time—I'd been embarrassed that she'd seen my secret shame. I hadn't written beyond a few pages of a new book in over five years. Paralyzed by fear, or others' expectations, or lack of discipline, or whatever.

It sure wasn't because I didn't have any ideas. At last count there were over two hundred beginnings of stories on the laptop that now glowed in the dim light of my office.

With one more glance at Syd, and again thinking she probably needed sleep more than she needed me pawing at her again, I opened a new Word doc and typed the words I'd typed nearly every workday for the past five years. Chapter One.

Syd let out a little murmur in her sleep and I pulled my fingers from the keyboard like I'd been caught with my hand in the cookie jar. She turned slightly, burrowing deeper into the old, soft couch. It was a great couch, and I'd taken a few naps on it. But its stock had skyrocketed today. Maybe I'd even see if they'd let me buy it and take it with me at the end of the year. It would fit, just barely, in my already-cramped office in my already-cramped apartment.

Taking my gaze from Syd and returning it to the blinking

cursor (damn that thing taunted me), I was about to start the first line of a new story, when I stopped.

I sat back in my chair, my heart beating a little faster, my palms becoming sweaty. I took a deep sigh, glanced at Syd once more to make sure she was sleeping and wouldn't witness what might quite possibly be an epic fail, and one that would end in another tantrum, or worse, tears.

I closed the new doc, not saving it, and went to the *Down In Flames* folder, opening both the notes Syd had transcribed about Esme/Rachel's story and the book file itself. I read through what I had written long ago, liking it. And then typed the words I hadn't in so long.

"Chapter Two."

TWENTY ONE

Syd

I WOKE UP TO SEE BILLY at his desk, hunched over his laptop. I watched for a moment from the couch, loving the feel of his coat on my body, and his scarf across my shoulders. I stretched, my body aching in several delicious places, and still he kept typing. And typed. And typed.

God, he was writing! I don't know how I knew, but I did. I totally sensed it. He was writing. And from the look of determination on his face, I'd guess he'd been doing so for a while. I leaned over and grabbed my phone from the floor where it must have fallen when I was hurrying to get my clothes off of me, and his hands on me. Three-thirty in the morning. My guess was that I'd dozed off around midnight. I didn't know if he had slept too, but if not, he'd been writing for quite some time.

He could have been writing every day for the past month I supposed, but I didn't think so. If I had to guess, I'd say that Billy Montrose was on his first real writing jag in five years.

I didn't slide off the couch and elbow crawl my way across the floor, or anything, but I was quiet as I left the couch and put on my clothes. I could tell he saw my movement—there was a tiny flinch in his jaw—but his fingers kept flying and I kept quietly putting myself together.

I would have loved to watch him work all night long, but I sensed this might be a pivotal moment for him, and I didn't want to impose, even as close as I felt we were. I guess you didn't get much closer than him being inside me.

No, that wasn't true. I'd had sex with boys with whom I'd never felt close to. In fact, I'd *only* had sex with boys for whom I had no feelings.

But that had been before. Now that I knew what it could be like with someone you liked, admired, respected and…okay, loved, I could never go back to casual hook ups just to feel good, or worse, sleep with someone with the hopes that they'd like me more.

No. Never again. I knew it would end with Billy after the semester, but that was okay. Tonight he'd given me a gift much more precious and valuable than the beautiful scarf.

Fully dressed, I made my way to the desk. As I approached, Billy finally fully noticed my movements and he looked up, a distant look in his eyes. His focus came back on me, and he smiled. "Hey, did I wake you?"

I shook my head. "No. I need to get going."

He looked at his laptop with a look of regret. "Sure. Let me walk you home." He started to rise, but I waved him to sit, which he did.

"No, it's fine. It's not that far to the dorm. And nobody's out. I'll be okay."

He started to argue, but I kept going. "Besides, you can't really be seen walking me to my dorm in the middle of the night. I have my pepper spray." He smiled. "And don't forget, I come from the mean streets of Queens. I can handle myself."

He laughed, the sound loud when we'd been speaking so softly. "I'm sure you can. And, you're right, I probably shouldn't be at your dorm. I'm sorry about that."

Not wanting to start the whole "this is wrong" conversation again, I quickly said, "No worries. You keep working."

I rounded to his side of the desk and as I did, he lowered the lid on his laptop, then smiled at me sheepishly. "Sorry. That was just instinct. I usually don't let people—"

"Shhh," I whispered as I leaned over him. "I understand. But I just came over to say thank you for this." I wrapped the scarf he'd given me around my neck a couple of times. "And to give you this." I bent down lower and pressed my lips to his.

Immediately the embers sparked to flames and he reached for me. As easily as I could have slid onto his lap and taken off the clothes I'd just put on, I didn't want to mess with his flow. Or be the reason he stopped. I slid out of his reach, but he grabbed an end of the scarf and held on.

Sliding the luxurious material between his fingers, much like he'd done with my hair earlier, he said, "I like how this looked before better." Looking at me with animal desire in his eyes, I had to step back or I knew I'd be on top of that desk in seconds, his laptop long forgotten. Part of me really wanted that. But the part that loved Billy Montrose wanted him to keep on writing, more.

At least this time.

He let go of the scarf and I smiled, silently promising him there would be many more nights where he would be able to see me in nothing but the unique garment.

"Text me when you get to your dorm. If you haven't texted in fifteen minutes, I'm coming after you."

"I will," I said. As I pulled my coat off the hook he again made to rise, but I motioned him to stay. I pointed to the closed laptop. "Open it," I said as I unlocked and opened his office door. He did. "Write."

He smiled at me, and after I shut the door behind me, I stood in the deserted hallway a moment and listened. It was hard to tell for sure, but I was pretty certain the clacking of keys began right away.

I walked back to Creyts not even noticing the fierce February wind.

After I texted Montrose that I was in my room and he responded, I took a long shower, put on my pajamas and left the door to my room from the bathroom open. I was unpacking my bag from the day at my desk when I heard Jane shuffling into my room.

"Hey," she said as she entered. She was bundled up in her comforter and she crawled onto my former roommate Megan's unused bed.

Megan had gone home to Nebraska after the first week because her mom had died. She'd hoped she'd be back for this semester, but she hadn't shown in January. At first I'd texted with her a little bit, but I hadn't heard anything in a while. I wanted to reach out, but I was also trying to respect her privacy. I had barely gotten to know her before she was gone. I knew if it had been me, and my mother had died, I'd be at home now taking care of Duncan and Liam. There was no way my stepfather would have let me go back to school.

I'd waited for Housing to move someone else into our suite, but they didn't, even with Megan not coming back for second semester. So, her bed was mostly a gathering spot for Jane and/or Lily when they came over to my side of the suite. Sometimes I was really grateful to have the room to myself, often times I truly missed having company, even though Lily and Jane were just a bathroom away.

"Hey," I said back to Jane as I laid the scarf over my coat, my fingers stroking the fabric. "Sorry I woke you."

"You didn't. Or I don't think you did."

I felt bad about bailing on Jane tonight, but I could see

that under her comforter she was still dressed in leggings and a top. "Were you out?"

"No, I stayed in."

"Sorry I had to work," I said. Pulling back my wet hair into a ponytail, I moved over to my bed and climbed in. "Lily with Lucas?" I asked. Jane nodded. "That's nice, that he was able to get Valentine's off and that they can be alone together," I said.

"I guess," Jane answered, shrugging. Unsentimental as always.

I thought about Lily and Lucas out tonight. He'd probably taken her out to dinner. Maybe they'd gone somewhere else after for dessert or dancing. I knew I would never have that with Billy. I wouldn't have traded the past few hours for anything, but to have him look at me like he had, but over a candlelit dinner in some restaurant would have been nice too.

I sighed and stretched, placing my arms over my face, trying to blot out the thoughts of the road blocks that Billy and I would face for the rest of our time together. "It's so easy for them, hey?" I said, thinking again about Lily and her boyfriend. "They both know they love each other. There's no drama. No should-they-or-shouldn't-they. It's nice, right?"

I could feel Jane's eyes on me, but I kept my face covered. "Well, it wasn't easy at first, remember?"

That was true. "But it was never because she didn't trust her feelings, right? It was just shit that got in their way," I said.

Jane didn't answer, I guess caught up in her own thoughts.

"It's just so hard, you know," I said. I wasn't really talking about Lily anymore, but I didn't let on about that to Jane.

We lay in silence for a bit more, then I heard Jane get off Megan's bed (I still thought of it as her bed) and make her way to the connecting bathroom. "This new?" she asked.

I looked up and saw her holding the scarf. I nodded, and

willed my body not to blush. "Just got it," I said. It was true, but I knew the answer was nondescript enough that Jane would figure I'd gotten it in the past few days. I propped myself up on my elbows and watched Jane hold the scarf that had recently kept me warm after Billy left me sleeping on the couch to start writing.

"It's beautiful," Jane said, sounding sincere.

"Thanks," I said. Jane held it up to the light, then draped it back over my coat on the chair. The colors shone more brightly in this light than the dim desk lamp of Billy's office.

"Good thing you picked up a second job," Jane said as she turned to leave.

I wanted to tell her to stop so I could tell her everything. I wanted someone else to know of my joy, and yes, my confusion over my feelings. I wanted to tell her that my second job was the best thing that had ever happened to me, and that the scarf wasn't a purchase of my own, but a gift from the man I'd loved for five years. To tell her that he'd thought of me while skiing in Switzerland and had held the scarf against my quivering skin only hours ago.

But of course I couldn't tell Jane any of that. Nor Lily. And certainly not my mother, or anyone else back in Queens.

Montrose was mine, at least for the semester. But he was also a secret.

"Yeah, good thing," I said quietly as Jane walked out of my room.

TWENTY TWO

Syd

IT WAS, ONE HUNDRED PERCENT, the best month of my life. We fell into a comfortable routine. But unlike before when our routine consisted of avoiding each other's presence, now it was built upon being near each other any chance we got.

I would nearly run to Snyder Hall when I was done with either classes or my shift at the admin building, depending on the day. I'd work on the many boxes he'd bring over from his apartment while he was either still teaching or reading his students' papers.

If I was sorting piles of notes, he'd sit behind his desk to read. If I was transcribing, he'd read on the couch and I'd take his desk.

We'd keep the office door open when we were both working to ward off any gossip and in case students wanted to consult with him. He had standard office hours, but Montrose liked to be accessible to students. Not for the first time, I thought he made a good teacher, and that it was too bad that this gig was only for one year. I thought about that part, about him only here for a year, a lot.

Most days, I'd leave and meet Lily at the caf for dinner. Jane was still MIA most afternoons and evenings, though

I guess she could have been in the room all the time and I wouldn't have known it. There seemed to be an air of secrecy about her, when I did see her.

I didn't try to break through it, having my own secret to protect.

Billy and I had decided to keep the boxes coming here and not to have me work out of his apartment. For one, we knew we'd probably be a topic of rumors for just me working for Billy, we didn't want to add any fuel to that possible fire by having someone see me coming or going to his home. Bribury was a small school, and there wasn't one female on campus who didn't know who Billy Montrose was, whether they'd had his class or not.

For another thing, the old leather couch was temptation enough to quit early each day, we didn't need the added risk of a full-sized bed nearby. We'd never get any work done.

Not that the couch was the only surface in his office that we'd take advantage of as soon as I'd get back from dinner with Lily. The desk, his chair, the guest chair, the credenza... They all saw their fair share of action.

And the floor. Oh, the floor. One evening I had piles of his notes all around me, when I heard him leaving his chair. Brushing past me, he quickly closed and locked the door, turning off the overhead light, leaving just the soft glow of his desk lamp.

I looked up at him, a question in my eyes. My body always heated up the instant he shut the door and locked it, because I knew that soon he would be touching me, making me melt, making me feel special, making me...his.

But usually he'd wait until I'd packed up for the day, or was done with a particular box, not when I had notes scattered in various piles all around me.

He stood with his back against the door, staring down at

me. The lamp seemed to reflect off his eyes and it was easy to see the desire there. The desire I saw every time we were in this office.

"Ever since that first time we talked on the phone and you said you were working on the floor. And then you stretched out. It was before we FaceTimed, and I only heard your voice, but I imagined you stretched out here, my work, my characters, my thoughts spread around you… It was just such an awesome vision."

"I remember," I said, my voice rough and deeper than normal.

He pushed away from the door and went down to his haunches.

"I never forgot," he whispered and crawled to me, papers crinkling under his knees, skittering away under his hands as he made his way to me. "Do it," he said. "Lie back."

I did. And it was crazy erotic having Billy Montrose make love to me on his office floor with the sound of his life's work crunching around—beneath—us.

It was later that same night, as he was helping me clean up the mess we'd made (and had no guilt whatsoever about) that I came across notes about Aidan Colly for a book just named *GP* in his notes. I recalled a *GP* folder from the day I'd opened all his docs, but it was one I hadn't gotten to before he came in and blew a nut.

"Aidan Colly?" I asked him. "You're doing a sequel?"

His face, so clear and at peace moments ago when he'd been inside me and looking down into my eyes, turned troubled, and I instantly regretted the enthusiasm that must have been in my voice. "I didn't think I'd seen any notes on a sequel before," I added, looking around, putting a no-nonsense tone into my voice. Like my heart wasn't pounding with the thought that my author lover was going to continue on with my favorite literary character ever.

"There aren't many," he said. His hands stilled on the papers he was collecting and he placed them on the carpet, then stood up, zipping up his cargo pants as he did. He crossed to his desk and sat down as I continued on with the reorganizing. I didn't like that he'd pulled away, but honestly, I wanted to put the papers back in the order I wanted. This was *my* giant jigsaw puzzle after all.

I waited for Billy to come to terms with whatever ghost Aidan Colly represented to him. And to talk about it with me.

"It seemed the easiest route to go at the time. It wasn't what I necessarily wanted to write next."

"No?" I said, but kept my attention on the work, not looking back at him.

"No. In fact, I think I started *Skylark* first. But then *Folly* hit and everybody loved Colly, and I knew I could clean up with a sequel. I didn't know at the time how much money I would end up seeing with *Folly*, so that was foremost in my mind. I wanted to be able to support myself as a writer."

"Well, you've accomplished that," I said lightly.

"Yeah, I have. So far."

I thought I'd lost him, but I kept on working, letting him sift through his demons like I sifted through his notes.

"When we sold *Folly*, my agent insisted on a one-book deal, even though we got offers for two, and even three books. She said because of the price that *Folly* went for at auction, that the publisher would put so much promo behind it that it couldn't help but do well. And then we could negotiate for a killer deal for the next book."

"Sounds like she was right," I said, my back still to him.

"She was. It's not her fault that I haven't been able to cash in on that by completing a second book."

"Is that when you switched from *Skylark* to the sequel?"

The piles were all straightened and I turned to face him, though I stayed seated on the floor. I had put my clothes back to rights, but I knew my hair and swollen lips showed the past hour we'd spent in each other's arms.

But he wasn't looking at me. His gaze was fixed out the window, even though the shades were down.

Slowly, he began to nod. Still looking at the window he said, "Yes. We weren't counting on *Folly* doing so well with the critics. We knew it would do well the first few weeks out because of what the publisher was putting behind it, but then…once more and more big-hitter reviews came in…"

"You moved to the sequel. *GP?*"

"*Gangster's Providence.* But I didn't get very far."

"No?" I asked, though his number of files on his computer was answer enough.

He shrugged, and his gaze finally fell to me. "*Folly* was a coming-of-age story. How many times does someone come of age?"

"I don't know. It seems like it could be once. Or for other people, it could be all the time. People change. What they grow into changes." I looked away from him, his gaze was too intense. It felt like he knew more secrets than I had revealed.

Would ever reveal.

"Yeah, that's true. But, I didn't want to do that to Aidan. I left him in a good place at the end of *Folly*. And yes, other challenges will most certainly come his way, but I didn't want to manufacture them just to cash in on him. It sounds crazy, but it kind of felt like I was…betraying him, you know?"

I nodded. Yeah, I did know. Though I—and any other Billy Montrose fan—would love to read a *Gangster's Folly* sequel, I did kind of like the idea of Aidan Colly staying forever as we left him.

"Anyway, I knew it didn't feel right, and I never came up

with much. I put the idea away for a while, and tried to go back to *Skylark*, but by then… I don't know. I lost the thread or something."

He looked away from me with a sad smile. "And thus began what I now call my Years of Starts." He motioned to the completed boxes in the corner of the office and the remaining ones on the credenza.

I'm not typically the pep talk kind of girl. That is much more Lily's area. I kept my voice equal, without any sign of rah-rah, and said, "And this will be your Year of Finish."

He looked at me for a long time. I held his gaze, not saying a word. This was on him. I could lead the author to water…

"Yes," he finally said. "It will be."

We both took deep breaths, like something monumental had just been overcome.

Montrose pulled his laptop over to him and opened it up. And I pulled the *GP* notes over, and immersed myself in my other boyfriend—Aidan Colly.

TWENTY THREE

Montrose

IT SEEMED SO WEIRD to be writing without Syd in the office. It was startling to realize just how much I'd become used to hearing her papers rustle, or the soft clack of her keyboard as I read students' papers or—wait for it—started a new chapter in my work in progress.

Yeah, I was deep into *Down in Flames*. I was still on the fence about the whole Esme/Rachel thing, so I was just using Esel as a placeholder knowing it would be an easy find and replace later.

It wasn't quite as inspired as *Folly*, and the writing didn't flow. It was…work this time. But it felt good to keep going on the same project, and I tentatively held my literary breath that perhaps I was past the big hurdle in my career.

Something wasn't quite right with it, though. There was something missing. But, where before my mind would have wandered to other stories, other characters, this time I stuck it out with Esel and crew, and trudged through. I trusted myself as a writer enough (okay, almost enough) to know I could figure out what was missing by the time I finished the first draft and could go back and fix it in edits.

My phone rang and at first I got excited thinking maybe

Syd's roommate's birthday party got over early, but realized it wasn't her ring tone.

"Hi Nora," I said to my agent.

"Hi Billy, sorry to call you on a Friday night."

"That's okay, I'm actually still in the office."

"Great. So, how's the writing going?" she asked, just like she had every time she'd called me in the past five years. First it had been weekly, wanting to cash in on the post-*Folly* buzz. Then it had dropped to every other week, then monthly. Now I heard from Nora about four or five times a year with a "I'm ready anytime you are, Billy. People will be jumping to get your next book…they just won't be jumping as high next year."

I could only imagine how much money I'd left on the table by not having a second book finished in the first year or two after *Folly* came out.

Those thoughts will only impede your journey forward. My shrink's voice played in my head as I gauged how much to share with Nora.

"Well, Nora, it's early, but I think I'm on to something."

There was a long pause on the other end. I'd said stuff like that to Nora early on, but after a while I had figured there was no sense fudging the truth—or outright lying—to the woman who had a stake in my career.

"Billy…that's…that's great," she said, genuine enthusiasm, and surprise, in her voice. "How far along are you?" the businesswoman in her asked. No "What's it about?" or "Are you liking it?" Nope, those were questions from an editor, or a fan. My agent was one of the best in the business and I valued her greatly. But she was not a cheerleader or a hand-holder. Something that appealed to me when I signed with her.

I did a quick look at my word count, something I had refused to do thus far. "I'm at…" (holy shit) "a little over eighty-thousand words." *Folly* had been right around a hundred thousand words. And though *Down in Flames* would probably be a bit longer, it wouldn't be a lot over that. I wasn't far from being done with the first draft. (Holy shit!)

Another long pause. Nora was probably quickly trying to process this news. I'd never given her anything more than "I'm a couple of chapters in," and even that had been a lie.

"Billy, that's great," she said, her voice still unsteady, as if she was sailing in uncharted waters. I'm sure she got "almost there" type of news from her authors all the time, but in the six years I'd been with her, she'd never heard it from me. *Folly* was complete before I submitted to agents way back when. I'd done some polishing based on Nora's notes before she'd shopped it, but this was new territory for the two of us together.

"Um…well…I know you've been reluctant to show me anything you were working on in the past, but…"

That was because there was never anything beyond chapter one. But, still…I wasn't sure I was ready for feedback yet. At least not from my agent. "I don't think it'll be too much longer before I can send you the completed first draft. That might be best."

"Of course. Really, you think you'll…complete it? Soon?"

I laughed at Nora's inability—even being the shark that she was—to hide her shock.

"Yes, Nora, this one *will* be completed. And if I can get a couple of glitches figured out, it will probably only be three or four weeks. Of course, there will be edits and—"

"Oh, my God, Billy! That is such great news." Nora had been a great agent for me, leading me through the process of first time publication with tough love, but patience. To now hear what sounded like tears in her voice…it made me feel both joyous and shitty that it had taken five years to get to this point.

Let the rest of the bullshit go. I'd said to Jane Winters. *That's all behind me. It was all…pre-Syd.*

I was vaguely paying attention as Nora went on and on about her game plan for the book. I made the necessary noises, but my mind wandered to Syd.

I had thought that Bribury was what I needed to kick-start my writing, at the very least to get out of NYC and the various distractions the city held for me.

But I'd been at Bribury for a semester and had never even come close to typing "Chapter Two."

It was only after working with Syd, talking with Syd, making love to Syd, that things became…unclogged, and I was able to let my thoughts flow freely on the page.

As if I'd conjured her up, there was a knock on the door and she stuck her head in. Seeing I was on the phone, she started to back out of the semi-open door, but I motioned her in. She waved to me and then proceeded to take off her coat, boots, hat and mittens.

"Okay, Nora, that all sounds good. Hold off on anything concrete, though, okay?" I said, not really having heard all she'd said. Certainly nothing since Syd had taken off her coat and I saw she was wearing those skin-tight, stretchy legging things that all the Bribury girls were wearing. Syd had on a long sweater hiding all the best parts, but I knew very well what I would find underneath that bulky, black wool. And I'd soon be refreshing my memory.

"Okay, sure," Nora said, drawing my mind back to the conversation. But my eyes stayed on Syd as she took a pile of papers from the credenza and headed over to the couch with her backpack. "But, Billy?" Nora said.

"Yes?"

"How about I have some casual lunches and just let it… slip that you're close to being done. Just to, you know, get a buzz started. Would that be okay with you?"

"How long can we sustain a buzz?"

"For you? At least six months."

"I won't need six months. Unless you read it and think it needs four months of work."

I could tell she was wondering which way to go. Be prudent and possibly deflate me, or... "There won't be four months' worth of work, Billy. I'm sure it will be great."

Nora wasn't one of the top literary agents for nothin'.

"Okay, then. Just a casual slip. Don't let them think we're shopping yet. And make sure Adina is one of the people who hears the news."

Adina Saunders had been my editor with *Folly* and had really smoothed out my first-time edges and helped shape the book. Because of the deal we'd held out for, we didn't *have* to bring it to her first, but I wanted to give her that courtesy. I'd take the best deal for me and for *Down in Flames* (assuming I was offered any deal), but I wanted to give Adina a chance to match it so we could work together again.

"Got it. As it so happens, I'm having lunch with her next week."

"Great. Then hold off on any other leaks until you have lunch with her. Let her be the first to hear it."

"Will do. Are you sure you don't want me to take a look at what you've got so far?"

I swallowed, thinking. It just didn't feel right. "Nah, I'm good right now. I just want to finish it."

"Super. Okay, I—Oh, Christ, I almost forgot the reason I called you."

"What's that?"

"Well, I don't think it's anything to worry about, but we've been getting mail again from an overzealous reader. Another Folly Dolly."

"Kari Aldrich again?" I said, naming my most persistent

fan/stalker. I noticed Syd's head move when I mentioned another woman's name, but she didn't look up from her work.

No need, she had nothing to worry about. Crazy fan girls (who got absolutely no attention from me) aside, these days I wasn't looking at anyone but Syd.

"No, a new one. I just wanted to give you a heads-up. Her name is Sarah Tudreau. The usual kind of letters…'she feels she knows you' and 'she knows you're her soul mate.' You know the drill."

I sighed. "Anything I need to do?"

"No. We've sent her the standard letter. And are prepared to send her the more strident one if we keep hearing from her. It helps that you're not at your apartment. This one lives in the city."

Jesus. It was sad that we had levels of "Fuck off, Crazy" letters that we'd had to send to some people.

We'd even had to do a restraining order against one.

Women. Girls. They were all female, and all knew that we were "meant to be together" because they'd loved the character Aidan Colly and assumed he was me.

"Okay," I said. "Thanks for the heads-up."

"It's probably nothing, but I wanted you to know the name. Just in case she showed up on your doorstep or something."

"Yeah, I appreciate it."

"Okay. Keep me posted on your timeline and I'll let you know how lunch with Adina goes next week."

We said our goodbyes and I hung up. I stayed behind my desk, but said to Syd, still engrossed with something I'd written on a cocktail napkin, "I didn't expect to see you tonight. How was the party?"

She lowered the napkin, putting it into a pile next to the couch. One of several she'd already made since she arrived. The woman worked quickly.

"It was good. Lily and her boyfriend dropped me at the dorm. They were going somewhere to be alone, and Jane was staying at the Stratton's, so I decided to change and come over here and get a couple of hours of work done."

It was nearly eleven. I had been thinking about packing it in and heading home before Nora had called. Now I was happy that her call had made me stay until Syd arrived.

"Oh, I wanted to ask you something," she said as she extricated herself from the pile of papers on—and around—the couch and came over to me, pulling something up on her phone.

I rolled my chair back and moved my laptop over so she could sit on my desk and face me, as she often did when we were talking about one of my student's papers that I asked her opinion on, or one of my characters that she was working on.

My desk chair was kind of cool in an old-school kind of way, but with its high, curved, wooden arms, it wasn't ideal for her to sit on my lap, or straddle me.

Though we'd tried like hell a couple of times. We had kind of gotten it to a point though, if she straddled me, but put her legs up high, over the arms, then leaned back to the desk—

"Is this the guy from the wedding?" she said, holding a pic on her phone in front of me, pulling me from my carnal memories.

"What guy? What wedding?" I said, as I took the phone from her. She hoisted herself to sit in the space on the desk I'd cleared for her.

"From Betsy Stratton's wedding. The one who Jane kissed."

I looked at the photo. It was of Jane Winters in a green dress, looking very different than she normally did, standing next to a young man in a tux. I enlarged the photo to see their faces better.

It was obvious they didn't know Syd had taken the

photo—they only had eyes for each other. What may have begun that night on the dance floor of Betsy's wedding had definitely developed into something…deep. I almost felt like I was prying in on a very private moment.

"Yeah, that's him. His hair's not in the ponytail, but it's him." I handed the phone back to Syd who studied it again.

"Hmmm, the plot thickens."

She went on to recap Jane's party, which, for reasons Syd didn't know for sure, had been held at Caro Stratton's estate. A home I knew a little bit from when the gang would go for an occasional weekend away from Brown. It'd been a lot of years since I'd been there.

"It's all tied to Joe Stratton running for governor?" I asked Syd when she'd finished.

She shrugged. "I guess. There was a big undercurrent of secrecy all evening, but I wasn't sure of what. But, my take is that this guy—Stick is his name, by the way—is doing some auto mechanic work for Mrs. Stratton, and somehow met Jane and…I *think* they've got something going." She was still gazing at the picture.

"It would appear that way from the way they're looking at each other," I said.

"But why keep it secret?" she said, more to herself than me. She seemed to remember she and I were in a top-secret relationship, because after a moment she softly nodded, like she understood. She clicked her phone off, and put it down next to her hip on the desk.

"I wish…" I said, not really sure I could tell her everything I *did* wish about her and me. About us. "I wish we weren't secret. I wish I could have been your date tonight. Besides being with you, it would have been nice to see Caro."

Her legs swinging softly into the desk well, she said, "That's okay. It was really small. You didn't miss much."

I placed my hands on her calves, stilling her movement. "But…I'm sorry," I said, trying to convey my feelings of regret that we couldn't be public. That I couldn't publicly let the Bribury campus know that I was crazy about Syd O'Brien.

A student. And my employee.

She placed her sock-clad feet on my knees. "It's okay, I know the score," she said.

"Yeah, but…"

"Would I have loved to go to the party with you tonight? Yes. Would I like for my friends to know you're my—" She stopped, and chewed a little on her bottom lip, a mannerism she produced when she felt a little insecure. Yeah, I knew her *that* well.

"Valentine?" I finished for her. I was happy for her to call me anything she wanted, but of course she couldn't. At least not to anybody else.

"Exactly. That you're my Valentine." She smiled and I moved my hands up and down her calves. "But," she continued, "there is something kind of hot about the secret lover thing."

"Nah, it's just us. There's something kind of hot about *us*," I joked, but the teasing tone in my voice quickly died as she looked at me with those huge brown eyes.

Just as I was about to move her foot higher up my leg, she pulled away. "Unh-uh. I need to get some work done…first."

Happy to know there would be a "second," I let her go and watched as she returned to the couch.

I couldn't tell anybody how I felt about Syd. And, to be truthful, my feelings for her scared the shit out of me. I hadn't felt like this about anybody since Diandra. And what was especially scary, I was pretty sure I hadn't felt as deeply about Diandra in the several years we'd been together as I did about Syd after only months.

No, I couldn't publicly announce my feelings for Syd.

And, because I couldn't articulate them myself (some writer!) I couldn't even tell her privately how I felt.

Or maybe I could…

I put my hands on my keyboard and pressed the space bar, waking up my laptop to the *Down in Flames* doc I'd been working on when Nora called.

"Hey," I said, and Syd looked up with a question in her eyes. "How would you like to read something I'm working on? I'd like your thoughts."

I could tell she was trying to temper her reaction, to act cool about my offer, and I think I fell a little in love with her right then.

She put down the stuff she was working on and did a nonchalant stretch of her arms over her head, like she was getting ready to read just another box of my existential meanderings on paper. "Sure. Whatever. This pile can wait."

Yeah. Definitely a little in love. Maybe even a lot.

"Cool," I said, trying to match her nonchalance.

But my hand trembled as I did a keyboard command I hadn't done for anything original in…shit, I didn't know how long.

Print.

TWENTY FOUR
·⟨⟩·

Montrose

WHEN I GOT BACK with breakfast, she was still reading, though she'd moved back to the couch from the desk where I'd left her. I put a coffee on the floor next to her, noticing the pile of pages she'd already read was considerably higher than when I had left a couple of hours before to go back to my apartment and shower, then pick up some food for us.

Syd had been up all night reading *Down in Flames*. I'd tried to distract her with kisses and a neck massage, but she wasn't having it. She woke me up when I'd dozed off in my office chair, my eyes tired of looking at my laptop screen. I thought she was ready for a little round of nooky, or to even go home and get some sleep, but she only told me to move to the couch, then she'd taken up my spot at the desk and kept on reading while I slept.

It was Saturday morning, and though there had been a long line at the diner off campus, Snyder Hall was deserted. There might have been some department members in the offices upstairs, but the first floor was quiet. No students. Just Syd and me. And Esel, of course.

"Take a break," I said, as I unloaded my booty from the bags and spread it out on my desk. She held up a finger, like she'd be there in a second, but she made no move to wrap up. She did take a sip of coffee, and I waited for her to look at me, but she kept her eyes on the page the entire time, almost spilling the cup as she set it back on the floor.

It's what every author wants of course—to have a reader not be able to put the book down, to stay up all night reading. One of the best emails I ever received was from a reader berating me for making them lose sleep and call in sick because they couldn't stop reading *Folly*.

I ate my breakfast while it was warm, checked my emails, started reading students' papers, but stopped, realizing I wasn't giving them the attention they deserved.

Because all I could think about was what Syd was thinking. What part was she at? What did that clearing of her throat mean? Was it a piece of shit? And would she be able to tell me if it was?

Just when I thought it would be best to leave and come back later, she put down the last page in her hand. I would give her time to collect her thoughts, not pounce on her right away, though I desperately wanted to.

Shit, I always wanted to pounce on Syd, physically and/or literarily. And Literally.

She looked at me, her expression unreadable. Fuck, what did that mean? I could usually read Syd.

Not being able to stand it, I opened my mouth, but she held up a finger.

"Wait. Not yet. I…I want to try something," she said.

Try something? My throat was clogged with uncertainty and she wanted to "try something?"

"Okay," I said, keeping my cool, though I did think my voice might have cracked a little.

She got off the couch and walked over to where her backpack sat on the floor by the coatrack. After pulling out her laptop, and sifting through a bunch of flash drives she had in a side pocket of the backpack, she moved back to the couch, snatching a bagel from my desk as she passed.

"Mmm, good, thanks," she said, taking a bite and then booting up her laptop, and inserting the drive, as she sat on the couch. "This is all I want. You finish the rest."

I was stuffed from my half of the breakfast, but when I saw her start to work on her laptop, and then heard the printer a minute later, I dug into her breakfast with the zeal of a compulsive eater.

Comfort food for sure. But comfort from the unknown?

About ten minutes later she put her laptop aside, then came over and moved the guest chair in front of my desk over to the corner of the room. I rose to help her, even though I wasn't sure what she was doing.

"Sit, sit. I've got it," she said. "I just want lots of floor space."

"What'd you have in mind?" I asked, putting a lecherous tone in my voice.

She laughed (God, I loved that sound) and wagged a finger at me. "Not yet." Then she turned her back to me to get the papers off the printer. She looked over her shoulder, certain I was looking at her ass—which of course I was—then shot me a slow, sexy smile. "But soon."

I went hard, and only my writer's ego kept me from jumping up and telling her that my book could wait, and that we'd make better use of all that space on the floor.

Yeah, I wanted to know what she was going to do. Even more than I wanted to bang her silly.

At least, right now.

She spent the next hour taking pages from my manuscript that she'd dog-eared while reading, and spreading them out on the floor. Then she'd take a page from the ones she'd printed and intersperse them with the others, writing notes all over both sets.

I sat, mesmerized, but not saying a word. I didn't even feign doing any of my own work, just sat and watched as Syd worked. Her hair was loose this morning—she must have pulled her ponytail out at some point while reading—and it swayed against her back as she stretched to put different pages in piles. She'd created a circle around herself, with the papers on all sides of her, some two or three pieces of paper wide, creating a petal effect, as if Syd was the center of a daisy. No. With her coloring, it would be more of a black-eyed Susan.

She stood up gracefully, careful not to catch any of the paper. Hands on hips, she surveyed her work, turning slowly in a circle until she faced me.

"Okay," she said. "First let me say that *Down in Flames*, as you have it written now, is…" She took a deep breath and let it out. I knew mine was held, but I couldn't seem to exhale. Not yet. Not until she finished her sentence. "Brilliant." Exhale. *Big* exhale. "It's really…so, so good, Billy."

Really big exhale.

"I mean, your voice is there, for sure, but this is also new and fresh. It's not you just trying to recreate the beauty of *Folly*."

I put my hands together, lacing my fingers, so they wouldn't shake in front of Syd.

"You're being honest, right? I've got lots of people who will blow smoke up my ass, Syd, please don't be one of them."

She looked semi-offended, and then waved a hand at me, as if dismissing what I'd just said.

"Of course not. I mean, as your…Valentine, I'm gonna gush of course. But as your assistant, it doesn't help you to not tell you if there are problems."

I pointedly looked at the paper flower surrounding her. "And are there? Problems?"

She didn't break her gaze and said—quite professionally for a nineteen-year-old—"Not problems. An *opportunity.*"

I laughed. "You should go to work for my agent."

She smiled and beckoned me to her. I rose, somewhat hesitantly, and carefully made my way to the center of the flower. (Was that the pistil? I'd always sucked at natural science.)

She carefully stepped out of it on the couch side, as I entered from the credenza side.

She sat on the couch as I stood at the center. "Okay," she said, hands up, as if gentling a wild animal. "This is just a thought, an idea. Like I said, I love it already as it is, but something kept striking me as I was reading, and then it clicked for me."

I looked at the papers, trying to see, trying to guess, what she meant. "What?"

"You're using the secondary character Brandon as your Greek chorus, right?"

I'd stopped being impressed and surprised by Syd's knowledge of literary structure and devices. The way she'd broken down all my notes and cut and pasted them together when she'd put them on the flash drives proved time and time again that she was wise *way* beyond her years when it came to books and the way that a novel worked.

"Yes," I said. "Part Greek chorus and part voice of reason," I added.

She was already nodding. "Right. Exactly. And I kept thinking, 'this isn't a Brandon. This isn't a new character.'"

"It isn't? He isn't?"

She took a deep breath as she shook her head. "No. It's… Aidan Colly."

I just stared at her, then looked down at the papers again, too far away to read as I stood over them. My head came back up to see her watching me. "It is?"

She nodded. "It is. It's exactly the Aidan at the end of *Folly*, where you left him, having sort of figured it all out."

"Is that bad? I mean, will people just think I recycled one character and threw him in another book with a new name?" I knew I shouldn't worry about what other people thought about my work, but there would be a *lot* of scrutiny on this book since it took me so long to write it, and because of how well *Folly* had done.

"No, it's not bad. But…here's a thought." A huge, bright smile came across her face and I couldn't help but smile back at her, even though I was scared to death of what she might say next.

"What if it's not Brandon? What if it *is* Aidan Colly?"

"Like, find and replace Brandon with Aidan? Bump up his scene count?" It wouldn't be hard to do, but it felt kind of… false.

"Sort of," she said, then rose from the couch and walked the outside perimeter of the flower. "I think the thought of Aidan came so easily to me because I'd recently transcribed your notes for *Gangster's Providence*."

"Okay…."

She took another step around the circle. "And then I thought about the notes you'd started for *Providence*, and things clicked."

"Clicked?"

"Yep. As I was reading, there was something that was being forced. Like you were trying to fit a green triangle into a red hole."

"What?"

She waved a hand. "Like that little kids' game, with the pegs and holes and squares and stuff." I nodded, and she went on. "I know that feeling. I'm like the green triangle and Bribury is the red hole."

I wanted to ask her about that, to dig deeper, she so seldom talked about herself, but I only waited. Though I did file the thought away for later.

"Like here," she said and crouched down in front of one of the petals of paper. "Brandon is doing this while he's with Esel—cute placeholder amalgamation, by the way—but at one point for *Providence*, you thought Aidan would say *this*." She pointed at two of the sheets of paper and I squatted down in front of her, with just a paper petal, four sheets of paper wide, between us.

"*He* would say this to Esel. My thought is Aidan is your Brandon—your secondary character, your voice of reason and Greek chorus—but you use your notes from *Providence* to do it. To make him really Aidan, even give him a small character arc that you alluded to in your notes, here." She pointed to the petal in front of us and I read her printout from the *Providence* transcribed notes. "And here," she said, pointing again to a different petal. "And also here." Another point. Another petal.

My mind was spinning. I wanted to both scream with frustration, and plant myself on the floor and start scouring her notes and breakdowns.

I told myself to keep it together. We could not have another scene like the time I'd pitched a fit when I saw her reading all my chapter ones. We had come a long way since then. And I hoped that *I'd* come a long way in the arrogant asshole department.

"Listen," she said, rising and taking a small step back, and then another, leaving the flower altogether. "In case you want to freak out and don't want to do it in front of me, I'm going to go to the bathroom, and take a long walk around the building to stretch my legs."

I wanted to stop her, tell her to stay, but I just nodded. She was so much smarter than I was.

"When I get back, all you have to say is, 'thanks for the feedback, I'll think about it,' and I'll never bring it up again. We'll forget I even said anything about Aidan."

I wanted to tell her how great I thought she was in that moment, to give me a graceful out, but I found my throat wouldn't work.

She was at the door, opened it and turned her head to say, "The book is *really* good on its own, Billy. No one will be disappointed in it."

She left, shutting the door behind her, and I spent what turned out to be the next hour going through her notes.

When she stepped back into the room, my arrogant asshole was nowhere to be seen, and instead I didn't know what to tell Syd first: that I loved her, or that I thought she should seriously consider becoming an editor, her notes being that good.

But instead of either of those things, I just led her to the couch, sitting first, then pulling her onto my lap so that she straddled my hips and I could look into those gorgeous brown eyes and say, "Thank you," in a soft whisper.

When I felt her body relax, when she was certain I wasn't going to throw a hissy fit, I then added, "Now. Let's see about those pegs and holes, shall we?"

I flipped her down on the couch and all thoughts of Aidan Colly left me as I slid my body over hers.

TWENTY FIVE

Syd

WE SLEEPILY WOKE to find that Saturday morning had turned into Saturday evening, the office nearly dark, with just the soft glow of twilight leaking in between the slats of the closed blinds behind us.

It was mid-March and the days were getting longer, but from the number of times the old heating unit in Billy's office went on, I guessed it was quite cold outside.

I had my back to Billy's chest, one of his arms under my head and sticking out over the edge of the couch. His other hand drew lazy circles on my hip. The plaid blanket below us had a freshly-washed scent and I realized that he'd taken both of the blankets to his apartment and washed them recently.

The sweetness of that gesture warmed my heart and I burrowed in deeper to his chest, rubbing my cheek against the rough hair of his forearm.

"Thanks for doing what you did today," he whispered.

"The blow job?" I teased. "It was nothing. Especially considering how long you were down—"

"The notes, smart-ass," he said, gently smacking my ass with his hand. Which he then quickly soothed.

"Ohhhh. *That*. No problem."

"Seriously, thanks."

"Thanks for not freaking out," I said, most of the teasing gone from my voice.

"You certainly know how to…manage me," he said. Part of me loved that thought—that I knew him so well now, that I knew when to give him space. When to push, when to pull. It made me feel…safe to know I knew him at that level. And it was not lost on me that I hadn't exactly let him know me on that level.

As if he'd read my mind, he said in a lazy voice, "I get that you don't like talking much about your life before Bribury…"

I should have felt panic, put up some shields or something. But I was in Billy's arms and felt like, for once, I could be completely honest. That I didn't have to pretend to fit in with all the other girls at this school.

He had chosen me. Not one of them.

"Yeah?" I said, trying to convey openness.

"And tell me to shut up if you want…"

"Okay…"

"But you know so much about me, and I just want to get—"

"Billy, what?" I said, giving him a tiny jab with my elbow, which he greeted with an over exaggerated "ooomph."

"The night I was an ass—"

"Which night, specifically?" I teased. I tried to hold on to the levity because I sensed what was coming.

"Yeah. Ha-ha. I was an ass, but I seemed to hit a particular nerve in you. Was that just putting me in my place about my choice of words—totally justified by the way—or was it… more?"

I thought about just brushing it off. But Billy had, in a way, bared himself to me by letting me read *Down in Flames*, and by listening to my ideas. I wanted to do the same for him.

"I was raped when I was thirteen," I softly said. It was easier to say it facing away from him. He didn't say anything, just continued to stroke my hip, but the motion now seemed more comforting rather than seductive.

The sun had gone down completely now and the room was cast in mostly darkness, just the glimmer of the streetlights on campus coming through the shades. I enveloped myself in the shadows, and went on. "By my stepfather."

"Jesus," he hissed, but said nothing more. Which proved that Billy Montrose knew how to manage me as well—if not better—as I did him.

"He wasn't really my stepfather," I went on, growing braver now, and just wanting it out on the table. I didn't want any secrets between us. "Still isn't. He and my mother never got married, but he's lived with us since I was eight."

"Christ," he said behind me.

I shook my head, loving the strength of his arm under me, as if he was holding me up. "It didn't start then. Thank God. It happened when I was thirteen and my mother was pregnant for my little brother Duncan."

Nothing from Billy, and I forged on.

"It happened once. I told my mother of course. She said… she said that Steven had probably been drunk. That she'd talk to him and it wouldn't happen again. But that I absolutely couldn't tell anyone, or they would remove Steven from our house and then how would we survive with a new baby. She…" the words caught in my throat, still not wanting to believe her huge betrayal of me. Though, at the time, I wasn't able to process that—that she had let me down. My thirteen-year-old brain projected all of those feelings back onto myself. That *I* was the one at fault. That *I* would be responsible for the new baby starving if I said anything. That *I* must have done something to make Steven act that way in the first place.

"She didn't even seem *mad* about it. She'd pointed to her big pregnant belly and shrugged, with kind of a 'well, what do you expect, the guy's got to get it somewhere' look."

"Fuck," Billy whispered behind me, then brushed my hair over my shoulder and placed the softest of kisses on my bare nape.

"Yeah, fuck," I said. "The one thing that she did do was somehow get him to never touch me again. I don't know what she said to him, or what she threatened him with, but he stayed away from me. Still as mean as a snake to me, but at least—"

"He's still in the house? Still with your mom?"

"Oh yeah," I said, lifting a hand, waving it, and then dropping it, like it was a very breezy decision for my mom to keep her daughter's rapist in the house all through my high school years. "When she was pregnant with Liam a couple of years later I made myself scarce through the last few months of her pregnancy, and when I *did* sleep at home, I made Duncan sleep with me."

"And when you didn't sleep at home?"

Fork in the road time. Tell him everything and taint his vision of me? Or fudge over the truth and let him think of me as just another Bribury Basic who easily overcame a tough break in her early teens?

"Well, for the first year after the rape, I really acted out. Grades went down in school. I became sexually promiscuous. A self-destructive streak really took over."

"I would image that's common behavior after something like that. Especially if you weren't able to talk about it," he said.

"Textbook, actually. Which I learned later."

"I am so sorry that happened to you, Syd. I know I can't take away any of that pain, but, I…"

He didn't know what to say, and I didn't blame him. I just continued to tell my story. "A year into that kind of shit, when

I was fourteen, I was held back because I'd failed all my classes. They had me work with a counselor, Ms. Francis, and she…" How to explain how much Ms. Francis had done for me? And mainly by giving me one book to read. "She pulled me out of it. Really worked with me that year to make me see that it wasn't my fault. She tried to help legally too, but my mother called me a liar. They would have removed me from the house, but by that time I was so in love with little Duncan that I couldn't bear the thought of being away from him. I was doing a lot of his care by that point."

"Thank God for Ms. Francis," he said, giving me another kiss, this time on the shoulder. It felt good, warm and comforting.

"Yeah, she was great. I don't know where I'd be without her. My grades went back up. Skyrocketed, actually."

"Your true genius being unlocked by Ms. Francis."

"Well, she was wonderful, but the thing that really turned me around was a book she gave me. I really think reading that book was the turning point for me. I was so in tune with it, it spoke to me so much. It pulled me out of myself, out of my situation and allowed me to see life as it could be, not as it was. It, literally," I jabbed him at the use of that word, and he chuckled, "saved my life."

"Wow. The power of a good book, right?"

"Yes. It changed everything for me. I read it over and over, still do. And besides the book itself, it instilled in me my love of all books, which of course is a gift in and of itself."

"What was it?"

I took a deep breath. Another damn fork. In for a penny, in for a pound. "*Gangster's Folly.*"

I felt Billy's entire body stiffen behind me. And not in a good way.

"Seriously? My book?" he said, and moved to sit up.

A chill rippled through me, and not just because he'd removed his body heat. He slid to the end of the couch, and I pulled my legs from his lap and sat up myself, pulling the blanket around me, the end of it long enough to still cover most of Billy.

I loved his body, but I had a feeling we would need to be covered for where this conversation was headed.

As if he was thinking the same thing, he rose from the couch and pulled his jeans on in the dark. He tiptoed through the papers still on the floor and turned on his desk lamp, casting the whole room in a soft glow. He then returned and sat down on the arm of the couch, further away from me.

"Okay, let's…can we talk about this? My book?"

"Yes," I said, not really wanting to. But I'd said all I'd wanted to say on the subject of that bastard Steven, my heartless mother, and my long road to finding myself again. I'd happily talk about how much Billy's book meant to me, even though I sensed it probably weirded him out a little.

"I mean, I knew you'd read *Folly*, we talked about it when we were FaceTiming, but I guess I thought that was fairly recently. Like, because you were taking my class or something."

"Well, I did reread it right before fall semester started. Because I was taking your class." I rose from the couch and dropped the blanket, reveling in the soft moan Billy let out. I didn't hide myself from him as I dressed.

"Reread," he said from behind me. "You said you read it more than once?"

I fastened my bra and slid my shirt over my head. "Yes. Although not as often as that first year." I looked over my shoulder at him, trying to let him see the significance of what his words did for me back then. "That year when I was… recovering, I read it over and over. Probably twenty times."

I was expecting a softness on his face, a look of…*something* to tell me he got it. Got what I was trying to do. Thank him.

But that was not the look he had on his face. His gaze followed me as I, now fully dressed, moved back to the couch and sat on the arm opposite him, bringing my bare feet up to land on the place where our heads had been moments ago.

I shrugged while he continued to stare at me. "I've probably reread it a couple of times a year since then."

A strangled sound came out of him, part laugh and part…I wasn't really sure. His strong chest heaved with a huge breath and he put his head down. I admired his body in the dim light. The way his muscles bunched in his shoulders, the long sinewy arms that held me so tight. The hands on his knees, which had done indescribable things to my body all afternoon.

"*Gangster's Folly* saved my life, Billy," I said only loudly enough for him to hear me. Scrubbing his hand across his chin he looked up at me, and the look on his face made me flinch.

Pain. There was such…pain. It was almost as if someone had hit him. Or hurt him very, very badly.

"What…?" I whispered, but he held up a hand to stop me.

"One question," he said, and I nodded. "Did you come to Bribury because I was going to be here?"

It was complicated, and I tried to parse my thoughts on the best way to word it, but my pause, momentary as it was, was too much for him.

"You did, didn't you?" he said, the pain from his face now clearly in his voice. "Syd," he whispered, but it wasn't directed at me. Instead, my name floated in the air like some kind of smoke signal. But I wasn't sure what it meant. It was like I didn't know the code. There was something missing here, that I wasn't getting.

"That's not exactly how it happened," I said, about to explain that Bribury was in my final three, and that his being here seemed like more of a tipping point than a sign from above.

Although, that wouldn't be totally truthful—I had taken Billy being at Bribury for a year as a sign that it was the place for me.

But not in the creepy stalker way that I now realized he was imagining.

He was shaking his head as I opened my mouth, so I stopped. "I think...I think we might have found the straw that broke the camel's back," he said with such sweetness, such melancholy in his voice, that I instantly knew that I was going to walk out of this office no longer having Billy Montrose as my Valentine.

The pain wracked through my body, almost physically pushing me back so that I had to put my hand on the back of the couch to steady myself. But I kept my voice firm and unemotional as I said, "Explain that, please."

He didn't look at me as he rattled off points that I'd thought we'd come to terms with long ago. "You're a student. You were *my* student. You *are* my employee." He looked back at me, then hung his head and said softly, "And you're a Folly Dolly." There was such sadness in his voice that I had to stop myself from crawling across the couch and comforting him.

Yeah, comfort *him*, when I was the one getting dumped. And for what? Being a fan of his writing?

"What's a Folly Dolly?" I asked.

He waved a hand of dismissal, which then dropped to his thigh. The thigh I'd rested my head against a couple of hours ago after I'd taken him in my mouth. "Nothing," he said. "It doesn't matter."

As he continued, I looked away from him, toward the pile of papers I'd laid out earlier. Could this be about them? Had he held his peace at the time, but the more he thought about it, the more pissed he'd become thinking that a lowly college freshman deigned to tell him how to structure his story?

While I'd been drifting asleep in his arms, had he been silently stewing?

"I mean, it's just not healthy—you and I. And I might have overlooked that in the beginning because I, selfish bastard that I am, desperately wanted you. But, knowing your history, what you've been through, you deserve to be in a good, solid relationship. One that—"

"Are you comparing what we have with what Steven did to me?" I snapped at him, my head coming up from looking at my handiwork to meet his stunned face.

"No. No. Jesus, no." He was shaking his head. He raised a hand, as if he wanted to reach out to me, but instead he dropped it and rose from the couch, stepping to the other side of the arm, as if to distance himself even further from me.

Like just breaking up with me wasn't distance enough.

"I just think that maybe we need to end things now. There are only a couple of months left before I leave anyway. I want you to be happy, Syd, but I don't think I can give you what you need."

My mind was whirling with trying to figure out just what exactly was freaking him out. Was it me taking it upon myself to basically re-write his work in progress? The fact that I'd been a fan of his book before I knew him? Or the fact that I'd been raped? Or that I'd dealt with that for a time by sleeping around?

Christ, piled together like that, it was a wonder he'd want to be with me at all.

The shame I'd felt all those years ago came creeping back. I tried to stuff it down, but it wrapped itself around the insecurity I had about even being here at Bribury, about being where I didn't belong, and together they stood arm in arm and attempted to destroy me.

But I wasn't the person I was at thirteen. And I wasn't even the same scared, insecure girl who stood in front of a rack of combat boots only months ago.

In the end, it didn't matter which of the facts was the silver bullet in my relationship with Billy. The truth was I didn't even care.

He didn't want to be with me anymore.

Some semblance of courage and strength, which I hadn't even realized I possessed, bubbled up in me.

"Okay. If you don't want to be with me, I'm not going to beg," I said. I slid off the couch (that glorious old, creaky couch where I had learned what sex with someone you love could be) and started packing up my stuff, getting my socks and shoes on.

"It's just that I—" He thankfully stopped when I held up my hand, very Queens talk-to-the-hand style.

I had my stuff packed and my coat halfway on when I turned to him. Pointing at the box on the credenza I said, "How many more are at your apartment?"

He shook his head, bringing his focus back to what I was saying. Just like he used to do in class. My throat tightened as I remembered watching him speak to us three days a week. I'd had so much more than that these past three months.

And now I wouldn't even have that much.

"Umm…two."

I nodded as I slid my backpack strap over my shoulder. "Bring them in for Monday. We'll go back to the old schedule. I'll come in the evenings after dinner. After you're gone."

He nodded his agreement, and my heart, secretly hoping that he'd balk at that idea, broke a little bit more.

"I should finish up next week, or the week after. Then my work on the project is done."

"I can ask payroll to move up your last payment to coincide—"

"No. It's fine for the direct deposits to come on April and May first. Let's just keep it that way, even though I'm going to finish up early."

"Okay," he said.

He'd set up my employment with HR and payroll so that my two thousand dollars (what was left after taxes) was deposited directly in my bank just like my paycheck for my admin job.

It took away any awkwardness of him paying me directly each month. When we weren't...us, it allowed us to not interact, not see each other. When we *were*...us, it took away the dynamic of him handing money to the woman he was sleeping with.

"Syd," he said as I had my hand on the doorknob. I turned. "I'm sorry. So, sorry. The last thing I want to do is to hurt you. I..." He still stood at the couch, and didn't move closer to me. Didn't try to reach out to me, and he certainly didn't try to get me to stay.

The work he'd done, the pages he'd so eloquently written, stretched like a white sea of snow between us. As cold and frosty as the remains of Montrose and me.

Ha. How was that for a goddamned metaphor! I was learning from the best.

"Goodbye, Billy," I said and walked out the door.

TWENTY SIX
⋄

Montrose

A MONTH LATER I PUSHED "send" on the email to Nora with *Down In Flames* attached.

It had been a tremendous month writing-wise. In every other way I was completely miserable.

I'd freaked when I realized Syd had been a…superfan. I couldn't call her a Folly Dolly, even though I wasn't really sure what the difference was between her and the other women who felt they were destined to be with me because of a character I wrote years ago.

The difference was I was in love with Sydney O'Brien.

And there were lots of other things, too. For one, she'd never let on that she'd read *Folly* that many times. I'd played all our conversations over in my mind countless times in the last month and I was fairly certain she had never even mentioned that it was one of her favorite books.

And for another thing, she *never* initiated contact with me in any way. And, being in my class, she certainly had every opportunity. Hell, if I had been told I had a zealous fan in that class I would have pegged Jane Winters as it for sure.

I sat back in my chair at the kitchen table in my apartment and watched as the email to Nora chugged through. Even though Syd was no longer in my office in the evenings (or ever), I continued to work in my apartment, only spending time in the office for my official office hours and to pick up and drop off students' papers.

It was just too painful to spend time in a room that reminded me of Syd at every turn.

She had finished her work a couple of weeks ago, just around the first of April. It felt like a cruel April Fool's joke to see her note reading "last one" with a flash drive sitting on my desk. But it was no joke, and I realized that, even though Bribury was a small campus, there was a very good chance that I would never see Syd O'Brien again.

I'd had all the boxes with my original notes shipped to my parents' place. They were going to put them in storage for me. I didn't want to trash them altogether, even though Syd had transcribed every bit of them, and I'd backed them up on external drives, flash drives and on Dropbox. I still liked knowing they were there for me somewhere—five years of my life. Five tough years of floundering with ideas that wouldn't stop coming, and no focus or direction to do anything with them.

Syd had given me that. Or Bribury. Or time. Or just plain manning up.

But I knew…it was Syd.

I'd wanted to call her so many times in the past month. Or leave her a note on the desk. But then I'd look at the calendar and realize we only would have another couple of months anyway (and only a month by now), and I'd crumple up the paper, or put my phone down.

She was so young, so sharp, and the drive she had…Syd was going to go places. And I didn't want her making any of those life decisions based on me being in NYC.

The night we broke up, when she told me about her past…

My heart ached for her, for her thirteen-year-old self, for the woman she was becoming. I'd wished I could have taken on her pain myself. I'd also wished that I had half the guts that she did. Does.

And then I'd gone and caused her more pain. It was for the best, though. Or at least that's what I'd told myself about forty times a day for the past month.

My phone rang, jarring me out of my pity party. "Hey, Nora," I said when I picked up. "I just sent you—"

"I know. That's why I'm calling."

"That was fast."

"Yeah, well, I've been waiting five years for that email."

I laughed. "Hopefully it will have been worth it."

"I'm sure it will. Listen, Billy, I want to show this to Adina first as we talked about. I'm prepared to give her a week to make a preempt deal if you're okay with that. If she doesn't hit our number, we shop it all over and hope it goes to auction."

"Yeah, that sounds good. I'd really like to work with Adina again. So, what should we ask for?"

We discussed our magic number for a while and finally came to an agreement. I thought Nora was asking for too much, but she assured me she could get it.

It wasn't about the money for me, it never had been. I just wanted to be able to write. But the way publishing worked, the bigger the advance, the bigger the push a publisher made, protecting their investment. And I wanted this book to do well. Ego. Pride. Professional preservation. Whatever. It was very important to me that *Down in Flames* be read.

"Okay, I'm going to call Adina tomorrow morning and tell her we're sending it to her. And that we're offering her the chance at a preempt."

"You're not going to read it first?"

"Normally, yes, but I've had her salivating since we had

lunch weeks ago, so I'll read it while she does."

"Okay," I said.

"It's good, right? Strong? Do you think I *should* read it before I send it to her?"

I thought for a second. Thought about the hours I spent deconstructing Syd's flower of ideas. Everything had clicked after that. Her combination of *Gangster's Providence* into *Flames* was startling with how well it fit. It had been there all along, I realized, I'd just been too close to see it.

But Syd saw it. And had the guts to show it to me, even after getting involved before had turned me into a complete asshole and cost us a valuable month of our time together.

"Yes," I said to Nora, no doubt in my voice. "It's strong. It's good."

"Okay then, I'll let you know what I hear in a few days."

"Okay. And hey, if she passes on it completely she'll be discreet right? I mean, word won't get out that my *Folly* editor passed on my second book?"

"I thought you said it was good? Strong. Why would she pass? I can see not meeting our number, but passing completely? Not going to happen."

"Okay…"

"Jesus, you authors. So talented and yet so…" She caught herself. We had a good relationship, Nora and I, but she probably knew better than to call me out on my bullshit.

"Insecure? Neurotic? Completely self-absorbed?" I offered up the choices for her. All being completely accurate. At least for me.

"Yeah, that," she said laughing. "Okay, more later."

"Okay," I said.

"And Billy?"

"Yes?"

"Have some champagne chilling."

I hung up and thought about maybe taking her advice and getting a bottle of bubbly in case good news came. At the very least I could toast typing "The End" for the first time in a *long* time.

And then I thought about not being able to celebrate with Syd. And about the fact that she hadn't even read the completed manuscript, made possible by her brilliant ideas.

It wouldn't be the same. Nothing would be the same for a long time.

I crossed champagne off my mental grocery list, pushed my laptop aside and pulled over a pile of papers to grade.

TWENTY SEVEN

Syd

I WAS STANDING IN FRONT of Billy as he sat behind his desk. I'd received notification from my bank that morning that a direct deposit had been made. May first. My last paycheck, even though I'd finished the work a month ago.

And had finished with Billy six weeks ago.

At first it had been torturous. Never having told Lily and Jane about Billy in the first place, I couldn't turn to them to help me heal. So, I did what healed me all those years ago. I read. And read. And read some more. Basically anytime I wasn't in class, working or studying, I escaped into different fictional worlds, until I was finally able to see that spring had fully arrived on the Bribury campus, and that life would go on.

But I needed to wrap things up with Billy. I didn't want to leave it as we had. I'd texted him that I'd like to stop by his office for a quick word and he'd agreed.

Now, he waved me to sit in the guest chair and I did. I took a deep breath and tried to articulate the thoughts and conclusions I'd come to.

"This needs to be said. And it's not that I'm trying to get you back. Because, what the hell, you're going to be gone in a few weeks anyway. But...I need you to hear me. I'd *like* you to understand me, but I need you to at least hear me."

"Okay," he said. He came from behind his desk to stand in front of me, leaning against the front of his desk, his legs crossed at the ankles, his arms behind him. A casual look, but I could tell by the grey of his eyes that he was nervous.

He wasn't the only one.

But, I channeled my inner Celtic goddess of strength and got off my chest what had been weighing me down for the past six weeks. For the past four months, really.

"Yes, I fell in love with you…the writer, before I ever met you. But you must have had some feelings for me because of the papers I'd written for your class. You told me yourself that those papers were part of the reason you hired me."

"Yes, hired you. I had no preconceived notion of you… as a woman. As someone I would come to—" He stopped, ran his hand across his chin. His voice was lower, softer when he finished, "be involved with."

The words stung, mostly because I knew they weren't completely true. But what stung most was the word unsaid, the thought unfinished, changed.

Remembering those early days on the phone, even before we started FaceTiming, I challenged him, like he used to enjoy then. "Oh, come on. You probably had a hundred students last semester. You're telling me it was only *my* papers that showed you I could put five sentences together? I'll bet I didn't even get the highest grade in your class."

From the look of chagrin on his face, I knew I'd made a hit. "Grades don't matter with something like writing, you know that."

I tilted my head. "Says the man who has hidden for five years out of fear of being judged."

He waved a hand and his face turned hard, his cheekbones, usually so touchable, became edgy and sharp, and the grey of his eyes turned dark, as if they were storm clouds about to burst. "It was the combination of your writing and the fact that you referenced a lot of good literature. It was obvious you were very well read." His voice was low, controlled. His tone said he was done talking about this.

But I wasn't through. "Well, the same could be said about everyone with an office in this building, and the administrative staff to go along with them. I would just bet that Corrine Patterson would have *loved* doing this for you."

He glanced away and I knew I'd made another hit. Shit, a couple more and I'd probably sink his battleship.

"Christ, she would have done it for you, wouldn't she?" He looked back to me for a second, then down at his feet. Hit. "She's the one who even gave you the idea to have someone help you. She asked to help you, didn't she?" He continued to stare down at his feet. I stood up and put a hand to his chest, still so warm and solid like the first time he'd held me, right here in this small office, in this exact spot. God, how I'd loved how solid, how real, how…mine it had felt all those times. And now, today… It was still the same chest, his body heat seeping through his shirt and sports coat. But it wasn't mine any longer.

And I wasn't going to let him forget that it once was…and because he'd wanted me as much as I'd wanted him. That I was no Folly Dolly. (I'd Googled it. Wasn't impressed.)

"Didn't she?" I said more loudly, giving his chest a push, but keeping my hand on him, unwilling—unable—to pull it away.

"Yes," he said, still not meeting my gaze.

Hit. I visualized the smoke rising from the ship as it went down, Titanic style.

"So don't give me any crap about only lo—wanting you because of your book, or how you write. Or being a damned Folly Dolly. There's more to it than that, and you know it.

There *was* more to it." I gave his chest another tiny push, and then it was as if the weight of my arm, the weight of my feelings for Montrose, the depth of complications we had, were just too much to bear, and I started to drop my hand.

Which was quickly stopped by Montrose slapping his hand on top of mine, holding it to his heart. "Yes, okay? Yes to all of it. I read your stuff and it, I don't know, it moved me in some way. Little by little, paper by paper. And there you would be, in the front row, three times a week." He squeezed my hand and—finally!—looked up, his grey eyes still turbulent, his face still stony. He didn't like this confession, not one bit.

And I loved every word he would offer.

"And there you were, sitting with Jane and Lily." He swept his free hand in front of me, as if encompassing me. "Looking like…looking like…you," he whispered the last.

"I Googled you at the library the day after I finished *Folly* for the first time, when I was fourteen." It was probably the wrong thing to say. I was just feeding into his issues with me having been a crazy fangirl before we ever met. But it needed to be said, the point needed to be made. "I even got the librarian to print out your picture for me, even though I didn't have any money to pay for the copy." A tiny rising at the corner of his mouth, but nowhere near a smile, and certainly not the full grin he gave me months ago. "I didn't have many girlfriends, but those I did had their walls plastered with posters of hip-hop singers and movie stars, even some Justin Bieber."

"Jesus, no wonder you didn't want too many friends," he said, the corner of his mouth inching a fraction higher.

I didn't mention that it wasn't because *I* didn't want more friends. Friends who would ask questions about my home life. That would throw him back into my past, and I didn't want to go there again, except to tell him…"I didn't have posters on my wall. I had that one picture of you, from the interview you did with *The New Yorker*, propped up next to my lamp, held in place by my copy of *Gangster's Folly*."

"Syd," he said, caution in his voice, afraid of what he assumed was Folly Dolly possibly emerging.

But there was so much more to me—more to us—than some Dolly.

"I read *Folly* over and over, I told you that. And I would look at your picture after I'd finish, and think that I...*knew* you somehow." He seemed to get uncomfortable and I quickly went on. "And yet, I didn't know you, not really. And you did the same thing with me."

He quirked a brow at me and I tried to tug my hand out from under his, but he held on fast. That gave me the courage to go on. "Okay, so not for five years, and not as..."

"Obsessively?"

"Strongly," I offered instead, though he was probably closer to the truth. "But you were first...drawn to me because of what—and how—I wrote, and then by seeing me so frequently, like I did with your picture."

Now. Now a smile, though just a tiny one, and tinged with a little sadness. I'd take it. "Well, it might have been a little reversed for me, if we're being honest. I couldn't keep my eyes off you from the first day of class. I didn't read your first paper for a couple of weeks after that."

"Seriously? 'Cause like you said, we're being honest here."

He nodded, still holding my hand to his chest, the warmth enveloping me from both his palm and through his shirt, as somehow our hands had slipped inside his sports coat.

"Seriously. From day one."

"Not Lily? She's the one every guy went for when we'd go to parties."

He shook his head, the movement so tiny it was almost nonexistent, but I saw it. Felt it.

"Not Jane? Guys are drawn to her, though I don't think they even know why. And the way she would flirt with you—"

"Not Jane. You, Syd. You."

I could feel the lump in my throat as I swallowed, trying not to fall into his arms, to pull him close and bury my face in his strong chest. I wanted to get this out.

"So, yeah, that came first, with *both* of us. The initial attraction from the writing and the physical. But, those first couple of days, on the phone, without seeing each other? That's when I knew you were so much more than just the author of my favorite book."

"Even though we were basically talking about my next book."

"Were we? Really, that's all? I remember feeling like I knew you so quickly, so intimately, and not at all as just someone with a book to write." I flexed my hand under his, against his chest, and he flattened his more heavily on mine.

"So did I," he admitted softly.

"And what we've become since?" I asked, holding my breath. "What we were?"

He seemed to be searching for a word, the man who could string words together so beautifully and effortlessly.

"Real," I offered up to him. "It was…we were…real."

His Adam's apple bobbed as he swallowed hard. "You're speaking in past tense," he said.

"You put us in that tense."

Another tiny nod, though his eyes never left mine. I tried to convey the depth of my feelings with my gaze, but knew my plain brown eyes could never let him know how much I loved him. Him the man, not the writer, though the two were inextricably connected.

"I know," he sadly said. "But I think…Syd, I agree with everything you just said, and I'm glad you pointed it out.

But…"

God, the dreaded 'but.' I knew this was not going to go the way I wanted it to.

But maybe it was going to go the way it needed to.

"I think that's the tense we need to stay, for a lot of reasons. A lot of *other* reasons."

"Okay," I said, "I understand."

And I really did.

That didn't mean I could stop the tears from falling down my face and from doing what I'd wanted to do for the past ten minutes.

Hell, since I'd first seen him.

I burrowed my head into his chest, not caring that my tears were wetting his crisp white shirt, probably leaving mascara stains. He could afford a new fucking shirt.

"Syd," he whispered, finally letting go of my hand so he could wrap his arms around me and pull me close.

"Goodbye, Billy," I said, but put my arms around his waist, hanging on to him, like I'd never let him go.

I would, but just…not yet.

"Goodbye, Syd," he said, placing a soft kiss on the top of my head.

We stood that way for a moment, but it wasn't long enough. Finally I stepped back. It was important to me that I be the first to let go. I didn't say another word or look back at him as I left.

Walking back to Creyts I let the tears flow down my face, not worrying about what anyone might think if they saw me. That in and of itself was probably a first, and a cause for a small celebration.

Yes, I had grown up this freshman year. A new strength, a new sense of self, insecurities in check.

And a broken heart to go with them all.

TWENTY EIGHT

Montrose

"BILLY, THIS IS NORA. Are you sitting down?"

Well, shit. That could mean good news or bad news. I was just entering my office, having finished a class. "Yeah, give me a sec. I need to put my stuff down."

I heard a sigh from Nora. I'm sure she didn't mean that I literally needed to be sitting down. But I wanted to have a hand free to write details down. I threw my bag on the guest chair, and my sports coat on top of it. Quickly making my way around my desk and sitting down, I pulled out a pen, grabbed a tablet and put Nora on speaker.

"Yes, okay. Shoot." I looked down at the empty tablet and wondered how big of a space "no deal" would take up.

"Adina loves it. They met our price."

Holy shit. "They're going to pay *two million dollars* for a preempt?" The amount came out on a part choke, part chuckle of disbelief.

"No. *Three* million. She offered for it so quickly I knew that we could get more than what you and I were originally thinking. She came in at one-point-five with a first offer. I got her up to three."

"Christ, Nora, you're amazing."

"Just doing my job," she said, but I could tell she was particularly pleased as well.

"I...I'm...speechless," I said.

She snorted. "That's a first. Listen, they want to fast track it, have it available for Christmas gift season. She already has her marketing team working on a sales pitch for retailers. She's going to call you later today to talk cover art thoughts and edits. She and I are going to meet next week and talk a book tour and appearances. We're behind the curve for this season, but they don't want to wait. They know they've got a hit."

"Wow. They're really moving on this." It had taken well over a year from the time *Gangster's Folly* sold to it being on the shelves. Publishing was not a fast moving machine.

"They really think they can capitalize at Christmas. A great gift idea for anyone who read *Folly*, and all that."

"Great. Sure, yeah..." I looked down at my tablet. I'd written down "Three Fucking Million" without even realizing it. But it wasn't all about the money to me. "Did Adina like it?"

"Billy. She just paid three million dollars for it. I think she liked it."

"Well, there's a difference between knowing a book will sell well, and actually...liking it." God, would the insecure writer in me ever shut the fuck up?

"She liked it, okay? She loved it. She said if it were a person she'd fuck it. Happy?"

I couldn't picture Adina saying those exact words, or anything even near it, but I just laughed and dropped it.

After getting off the call with Nora I tried to do normal things, so that I wouldn't obsess about the book deal. There was a lot of work to do before I saw *Flames* on the shelf this fall.

I unpacked my bag, putting the new stack of students' papers on the credenza, now box-free. There were stacks of papers throughout the office in various stages of completion.

Some read and graded, but not entered yet, some still untouched.

I sat in my chair and looked around the tiny office. A room that had given me such joy this year. And also pain.

After getting some closure with Syd last week, it was easier to remember only the wonderful times in here when we would talk books, eat Peking Delight, and make love.

And this was also the room that brought me back to writing, and remembering that I *could* write a complete novel, not just a bunch of beginnings.

Because every good story had a beginning, a middle and an end. Even if I didn't want my story with Syd to end, it had to. It was just too hard. There was just too much in our way, not the least of which was I was leaving Bribury in two weeks.

Yes, there would be times that she'd be in the same city as me, but as she'd pointed out many times, her New York was not my New York. I just wished I'd realized it earlier.

No. No, I didn't mean that. It was worth it, even though it had been so hard. Yeah, definitely worth it.

I debated calling my parents, or my sister, to tell them about the book deal, but I didn't. I wanted Syd to be the first to know, but after we'd said our final goodbyes last week it didn't seem right. Besides, I wasn't sure how happy she would be for me.

I decided to settle in and grade some papers, but wanted to first grab a soda from the machine down the hall. When I stepped into the hallway, I saw Jane Winters walking away from me, toward the exit. Most of the Bribury girls all looked the same from behind—long hair up or down and straightened, those legging things, brightly colored running shoes and, now that it was spring, small knit tops and light zippered hoodies. But not Jane. You could easily pick her out in the sea of Bribury co-eds.

And Syd, of course. I'd know Syd instantly even though she tried to fit the mold.

Seeing Jane reminded me of Caro Stratton's recent passing and an interview that Caro, Joe Stratton and Jane had done, which I'd seen the other night. "Hey, Jane. Got a minute?" I said to her back, loudly enough for her to hear.

She turned, not looking shocked to see me. Yeah, she probably knew where my office was from first semester. "Sure," she said, then made her way back to my office and through the door, which I held open for her.

I watched as her gaze quickly moved around the room, seeming to take everything in. I'd bet not much got past Jane Winters.

"The 'Who I am Right Now' papers?" she asked, pointing to a stack of papers yet to be graded.

"What? Oh, yeah. Not as entertaining as last semester's batch, I'm afraid." Jane and Syd in particular had written really insightful pieces that I still distinctly remembered. I'd felt so strongly about Jane's that I'd talked with her briefly about it the last day of class. I'd felt so strongly about Syd's that I'd offered her a job.

I motioned to the couch, the guest chair still having papers on it, and Jane sat down. My leather jacket was on the arm, had been there for weeks, since it had warmed up and I'd stopped wearing any jacket or coat over my sports coat. I made to move it for her, but Jane pushed it aside. A piece of fabric had obviously been underneath and it fell to the floor in front of Jane. It was the scarf I'd given Syd. She must have left it one of the last times she'd been here and it'd gotten into a crack in the couch during our lovemaking. A burst of pain swept through me. I wanted to snatch it out of Jane's hands but didn't want to tip her off to anything.

Which probably wasn't going to work, given the way Jane

seemed to recognize the garment. Of course she did, she lived with Syd. And the scarf wasn't one that anybody else on this campus had. And certainly wasn't a man's piece of clothing, not with the feminine design. Then she brought it to her nose and I knew she was smelling Syd's perfume.

God, did it still have her scent on it? Now I really wanted to rip it out of her hands. She handed it to me, not saying anything (yeah, Jane Winters not saying anything!), but lifting an eyebrow at me.

Busted.

"It's, um…" Where to start. How could I possibly put my feelings for Syd into words? Me, who made my living by choosing words, who found great joy and solace in words…I just couldn't begin to explain to Jane what I couldn't explain to myself.

"Complicated? I'm sure it is," Jane said.

I looked down at the scarf in my hands and willed myself not to bring it to my nose in front of Jane.

"Don't worry about it," she said. "I won't mention that I was here…to anyone."

I nodded, getting her meaning. She wouldn't mention to anyone about Syd and me. And she wouldn't mention to Syd that she'd seen me nearly come to tears over a pretty piece of fabric. I put the scarf on my desk and turned back to Jane, attempting to put Syd out of my mind. Not possible, but I did want to talk to Jane about Caro.

"I saw the interview you did with the Strattons," I said. "And I was sorry I couldn't make it to Caroline's funeral." The truth was I had been so engrossed in finishing *Flames* that I wasn't aware of it until a few days later. I had gotten together with Jason for drinks a couple of days after the funeral, while he and Betsy were still in Chesney.

"It was a nice service," Jane said.

Jason had said the same thing. "I'm sure it was." I leaned against my desk and crossed my ankles. "I just wanted to tell you…and I know this sounds kind of…*trite* coming from me. But seeing you in that interview? I was really…proud of you, Jane." I meant it. When I'd watched it, I no longer recognized the brash and brazen girl who'd outrageously flirted with me last fall. Jane had…found herself, as I knew she could. As I had suggested to her.

"Thanks," she said. "Your words to me…they meant a lot. They really helped me out."

I think she was sincere. At least there was none of her old biting sarcasm or anything. "I'm glad," I said.

She nodded at the scarf sitting beside me. "Now maybe it's time to take your own advice? Make it less…complicated? 'Let the rest of the bullshit go?'" she said, throwing my words to her back at me.

"Yeah, maybe," I said.

After she left I sat at my desk for a long time. "Let the bullshit go", "Syd", "teaching" and "happiness?" all joined "Three Fucking Million" on my pad of paper.

As Nora said she would, Adina called later in the afternoon. I hadn't left my desk, hadn't graded any papers, or gotten that soda. Had just stared at the tablet and thought.

Could I let it all go?

Adina not only liked *Flames*, she couldn't stop gushing. Not one to interrupt a gush, especially about my book, I let her go on. We talked about cover art ideas, of which I didn't have many, but really liked the ideas she had. We then talked about her edits. She'd be sending me her full edit letter next week, followed by her marked-up copy of the manuscript. But she said, "It's not a long letter, Billy. And it's mostly quick fixes—a few things need a bit more explanation, some clarifications, things like that. We can talk about turn around time then, but

I think once you see it you'll agree that the changes are minimal and we can have this book ready soon."

"Okay. Yeah, it all sounds doable."

"Super. We plan on making the deal announcement this week. I'll work with Nora on that. We want to get the buzz started. So you'll probably want to get some statements ready. I know you're at that college place for a little while longer, but we'll have time to sit down and talk it all out once you're back in the city."

I didn't expound on her "that college place" statement. I didn't want to share my Bribury adventure with Adina. Or Nora. It felt special to me, private. But maybe I was melding my whole experience this year with my feelings for Syd.

Then a thought came to me. "When you make the deal announcement, are you going to put in a synopsis of the book, or just announce the deal?"

"Not sure yet. Why?"

"Well, as I'm sure you realized, I have yet to name my protagonist."

"Oh, thank God. I was so hoping you weren't married to 'Esel.'"

I laughed. "No, it was a placeholder. I'm back and forth on the name."

"Okay. If we do a synopsis, we'll do it without a character name. Keep it vague. That might heighten some mystery actually. Just make sure you have it before I get your edits back, we'll be going to galleys shortly after that."

"I'll have it by then," I said. We said our goodbyes and hung up.

She'd loved it. So had Nora. And Syd had loved what she'd read of it. It had sold for three million. Maybe I *could* get away with using Esme. Fuck the haters.

I remembered Syd's words about my original Esme/Rachel

character notes and how they compared to Salinger's Esme.

Practical. Unsentimental. Wise beyond her years. Very matter-of-fact. And yet you know she's going to rip your heart out.

I opened my laptop and pulled up *Flames*. Yep, a quick find and replace and I had the name of my protagonist set.

I looked at my tablet again, checked the time, then called Corrine Patterson to see if the dean had time to see me.

TWENTY NINE

※

Syd

JANE WALKED WITH ME to class one morning a few weeks after I'd seen Billy for the last time, which was unusual. I didn't think she even had class until eleven on Tuesdays.

She'd been dealing with her own stuff with Stick lately, and though I didn't know what all had gone down, there was a period in there when she was a total bitch to be around. I mean, way worse than usual. But, the last couple of weeks she'd been flying high and it seemed like they'd worked it out.

She'd even been on television. An interview she did with her father and Caro Stratton had aired and Jane was getting a lot of attention on campus. Which of course she hated.

The three of us had taken the train to Manhattan last weekend to shop and have a girls' weekend—part of Jane's birthday gift from her father and Caro. We'd done a bunch of shopping at Barney's for Jane's upcoming stumping on her father's campaign trail gig. But she'd also taken me to a cool vintage shop she liked and I'd gotten a few things.

I now wore my new purchases and was…okay with the fact that I didn't look like all the other girls as we walked across campus. In fact, I kind of reveled in it.

"Listen, I saw something online this morning, and I

thought you should know," Jane said. She shrugged. "Maybe you already do know, but my guess is the way you've been moping around lately that you're not in the loop much."

Ah, the reason for walking with me. "What did you see?" I'd tried to hide my heartbreak from Jane and Lily, because then I'd have to tell them about Billy. And I just couldn't. So, I didn't think Jane would be sharing with me something she'd seen online about Billy. Like he'd reunited with his lost love Diandra Scott and was now engaged.

"Remember our prof from last semester? That hottie Montrose?"

A cold wind swept over my heart. No. He couldn't have. "Yeah?" I said, trying to sound uninterested.

"I guess he sold his next book. Big time deal. Like a three million dollar advance or something."

Emotions rushed through me and I swallowed hard. He'd finished *Down in Flames*. He'd *sold* it. And for a huge advance, which would only be given if they'd loved the book and thought it would be a huge best seller.

Pride and elation ping-ponged in my heart. I'd known it the moment I'd started reading it. To know that the publishing world saw it too… My throat barely worked as I said, "Is that so? Good for him."

Jane gave me a sidelong glance and a snort, both of which I ignored. Did she know? Why else would she even mention it?

"You know, I finally bought and read Montrose's big, supposed masterpiece," she said.

"You did?" I asked genuinely surprised. "What did you think?"

She shrugged. "Meh."

"Meh?" I was shocked. I knew Jane and I had different tastes in…well, everything (except wanting to sleep with Billy, we'd once shared that), but how could *Folly* not have affected her? How could—

"I mean, I kept waiting for the gangsters to show up. There wasn't even one gangster."

Oh, my God. I stopped in my tracks. Jane had to be smarter than that. "Jane, the gangster is a metaphor. It's supposed to symbolize Aidan's—"

"Ha. Got ya," Jane said, nudging me and continuing to walk on while I stared after her. "I got the metaphor, Syd, I'm not an idiot." I started walking again, catching up to her. "And yeah, I can see what all the fuss is about. Is this new one as good?"

"I don't know," I honestly said. "I read about three quarters of it before I…we—" I realized what I had just admitted. I stopped again, and this time Jane stopped with me. She didn't say a single word, gave no sign of knowing that I had read Billy Montrose's newest book. But if she'd been fishing, I'd taken the bait.

There was such a look of understanding from Jane, and just a little sympathy too. I stopped trying to figure out how Jane Winters knew everything. Sighing, I said, "Yeah, I think it probably is as good. Maybe even better. But, I didn't get to finish it."

She only nodded. "Well, sounds like you'll get to right around Christmastime. Hey, I already know what to get you." A little chuckle, then she slung an arm around me, squeezed and we continued walking.

"Very funny," I said, but I knew I'd be the first one at the bookstore the day *Down in Flames* dropped.

When I got out of class I checked my phone like I always did and almost dropped it in shock as I saw a text from Billy.

Do you have some time this afternoon? I have one last piece of the project I need your help with.

Had he found another box? Had I messed something up? He'd texted a half hour ago, so I wasn't sure if he'd see my response right away, but I told him I could work this evening if he'd just leave it on his desk.

Can't with this one. I need to explain it in person. I'm in my office all afternoon. Can you make it?

God, just when it wasn't completely devastating to think about him. To see him again. In his office where we'd spent so many hours. But, I had been paid to complete this project for him, and I was eternally grateful for that opportunity. *I'll be there shortly. I'm nearby.*

Because of the money I'd earned as a literary assistant, I would be able to spend the summer here, and even take a few classes, so I could stay in the dorms. Mrs. Otterbein had said she could use me and I'd probably get nearly forty hours a week at the admin building for the whole summer.

When we'd been in New York last weekend, I went to see my brothers in Queens and to let my mother know that I wouldn't be home for the summer. It hadn't gone well with her, but it did look like she had stepped up—or perhaps my grandmother had stepped in—and Duncan and Liam were being taken care of. It had been great to see my little redheaded leprechauns and I'd brought them both Bribury sweatshirts. They'd cried when I'd left and then I'd cried the whole way back to Manhattan, but I knew I wasn't the only big sister out there who went off to college.

As I walked down the hallway in Snyder Hall, I was happy to realize that I hadn't even once thought about going back to the dorm to change into my more…Bribury clothes.

But yes, I did run a hand through my hair and put on some lip gloss before I knocked on his office door. I waited to hear a "come in," but instead the door almost instantly opened, as if Billy had been right there waiting for me.

It had been so hard to see him a few weeks ago when I'd come to tell him how I felt. This time…yeah, it was still excruciating, even if I had gotten myself kind of back on track emotionally since then.

"Hi," I said.

"Hey." He stepped back and I entered the office and had an overwhelming sense of déjà vu. Boxes were everywhere.

"Did you find another set of notes?" I asked as I moved into the room and he shut the door behind me. I heard the quiet snick of the lock and wondered how many times that sound had made my skin start to heat and my pulse race.

"No. These aren't notes. This is the stuff from my office. I'm packing it all up."

Oh, right. He'd be leaving soon. Duh. I turned to face him and said, "About the job?" just as he said, "You look different."

I raised my hand self-consciously to my hair, which I had stopped straightening recently. The loose waves had grown on me, plus it saved a ton of time in the mornings.

He took a step toward me. "I mean good. Different good. You look good." He ran a hand across his chin, a gesture so familiar to me that a lump formed in my throat. "Jesus," he whispered more to himself than to me. "And I call myself a writer."

The book. Yeah, that was safe. "I heard about your book deal. Congratulations," I said.

"Thank you. I wasn't sure if you knew. I wanted to call you when it sold, but…" A pained look came across his face. He looked tired, but I supposed wrapping up his classes, getting ready to move, and selling a book would tend to take its toll on a man. Tired, yes, but he still looked amazing to me. His hair was a little longer and I remembered how I'd liked to sink my hands in it right at the base of his skull. Now, my hand would probably come to the bottom of his neck.

Not that I'd get the chance to find out.

He wore jeans and sneakers, with a black tee that only seemed to bring out the grey of his eyes. He watched me look at him and I knew the heat I was feeling being this close to him was creeping up my neck. "So, anyway, the job?"

He looked at me a second longer, then seemed to snap out of it and bring his focus back. Another familiarity that was both sweet and painful to remember. "Right. Right." He moved past me and his bare arm brushed mine. "I have an early galley from my publisher that I need proofread."

"And you want *me* to do it?" He nodded. "Don't they do that for you at the publishing house?" I asked.

Another nod. "They do. But the final look is on the author. And I don't trust myself, having seen it so many times. I need fresh eyes on it."

"Not entirely fresh eyes," I pointed out.

"No, but I think you'll be surprised how different it is from the version you read."

A little tingle of pride rippled through me. "Did you use some of the *Gangster's Providence* text?"

A laugh, rich and throaty and so good to hear, came from him. "Oh, yeah. I used most of your suggestions. You'll see yourself all over this version, Syd." He picked up a huge stack of paper from his desk and walked toward me. It looked like an entire ream that you'd take out of the package and put in the printer, but when he got closer I saw that the outside margins were huge, with the text being the size of an actual book with page numbers and folios and everything, just centered on regular printer paper. This must be what a galley looked like.

I reached out to take it from him, but he held it back. "I couldn't have done this without you Syd. None of it. I mentioned you in the acknowledgements, but it will never be enough for what you did for me."

I was in the acknowledgements? I reached again for the manuscript, curious to see if acknowledgements were included in publisher's galleys.

"But you can't take it with you. I really need to have it in my possession the whole time. I had to sign a waiver and everything. They're really afraid of leaks before publication."

"You think I'd leak it?" I said, but he was already shaking his head.

"No. Of course not. But I told them I'd keep it with me at all times. They're being really paranoid about it. I guess there's a bunch of online leaks happening for anticipated books lately. Like the whole book, not just excerpts. Ebook pirating, all of it."

"Oh, okay. So, how do you want to do this if you need to be in possession of it?" God, was he going to sit here while I proofread? No way would I be able to concentrate on his manuscript.

"Well, do you have some time now? Why don't you take the desk and start in on it. I've got the last of my class papers to read, and I can do that on the couch." He turned and grabbed something from his desk. "Oh, here," he said, handing me my scarf. "You must have left this here that last night that—"

"Thanks," I said, grabbing the fabric from him. I'd known it was missing of course, even knew when I'd left it, having searched for it the morning after we broke up. There was no way I was going back and asking him for it, though it pained me to not have at least the scarf as a physical reminder of our time together.

"So…can you start now?" He didn't seem to be waiting for my answer. Moving across the room, he picked up a batch of student papers from the credenza and made his way to the couch, where he plunked down, crossing one long leg over the other, ankle to knee.

"Uh, yeah…I guess," I said and walked around the desk, then took a seat. He just nodded and then started reading, red pen in hand. Something was off about this whole thing, but I couldn't figure out what. How was I even a qualified proofreader?

I studied him for a while, selfishly soaking in the sight of him while he was distracted. When he looked up and caught me, I just held up the manuscript in a "yep, I'm gonna read it now" kind of way. He just gave a tiny nod then returned to the paper he held.

A galley apparently is exactly what you see in a book, just in loose-leaf form. The title page with Billy's name was first, followed by the copyright page. Next was the dedication, which was to his sister, and very sweet.

On to the acknowledgements. First his editor, then his agent. His parents were thanked. And then…

A special thank you to Sydney O'Brien, who worked as my assistant on this book. She offered great feedback, advice, ideas, and the occasional kick in the ass when needed. I smiled and read on. *This book would not have been written without her.* That was nice. And… *She certainly earned the right to have the* Down in Flames *protagonist named in her honor.*

Wait. What?

I quickly flipped to the next page in the stack.

Chapter One

Nobody had ever met a woman like Sydney Cassidy.

Same opening line I'd read two months ago, except then it had been Esel. When Jane told me about Billy's book deal I'd briefly wondered if he'd gone with Esme or Rachel, or something else entirely.

He'd chosen Sydney.

My head snapped up to find Billy staring at me. "Why?" I asked.

He put the paper he'd been reading down on the couch and rose, then walked over to the front of the desk, putting his hands down and leaning over so that he was at my eye level, the desk between us.

The desk, and a whole lot of other shit stood between us.

"Do you remember the conversation about my character being Salinger's Esme?"

"Yes," I said. It had been the first of many conversations about his characters. "Vaguely."

"You described her as, and I quote, 'Practical. Unsentimental. Wise beyond her years. Very matter-of-fact. And yet you know she's going to rip your heart out.' Sound like anyone we both know?"

"I…I…" I was speechless and by his smile, he knew it.

He leaned a little further across the desk. Still not touchable from where I sat, but maybe if I scooted—"I didn't write you, Syd, but your name fits this character. To a tee. And it was a name I wanted around me always." He pointed to his book. "It's not carved in stone, but it will definitely be in print and on bookshelves."

I ran his words (my words, actually) through my head. "But *I* didn't rip *your* heart out," I said.

He put both his hands over his heart, white and stark against the black of his T-shirt. "From the first, you ripped my heart out. I'm just so sorry I did the same to you."

He took a step back away from the desk and I held my breath. Was he going to go back to his couch and start reading again? Was I supposed to just thank him for naming a character after me and return to work? Did knowing his heart was broken like mine help?

"Did you even really need me to proofread?" I asked.

He smiled, but it was small and faint. "No. I just wanted you to see it before it came out. It was true that I'm not supposed to let it out of my possession, so this seemed like a good way to get you here."

Oh. So I wouldn't be spending torturous hours only steps away from the man I loved but who didn't love me back. I held back a sob, cleared my throat and said as I rose from my chair, "Oh, okay. Well, it was a lovely gesture, thank you."

A look of panic came across his face. "No. No, I didn't... Shit, I messed this up." I was rounding the desk now and he took a step over to stand in my way. "Syd," he said, and started to reach for me, when a knock came at the door.

His hands dropped back to his sides. "Are you fucking kidding me?" he murmured and left me standing in confusion as he went to open the door.

"We're here to move your stuff," came a voice from the other side of the door once Billy had opened it. From my angle I couldn't see the man.

"Now? This isn't a really good time," Billy said.

"This is when we were scheduled to be here."

Billy ran his hand through his hair. "I know. Well, I forgot actually, but yeah. Can you give me a few minutes at least?"

A pause, then, "We can do the office next to you first, but then we need to do this one. That's all for this floor."

"Thanks. Yeah, okay. I just need a few minutes is all," Billy said.

"It'll take us about forty-five to get the other office done, if that." Billy was nodding and thanking the man again. "Office two-thirty-three? That's the one you're moving to?" the man added.

"Yeah, I guess," Billy said. "I know it's two down from Corrine Patterson's."

"Yep, that's it. Okay, see you shortly," the man said and Billy thanked him again, then closed the door. He put his hand against the wall and took a deep breath, then turned to me.

"What's going on?" I asked. "They're not here to move your stuff to New York?"

The smile was back, but still so tentative. "No, not New York. They're moving my stuff to my new office upstairs."

I still wasn't getting it. "Seems like a stupid time to assign you to a new office, right before the end of the semester." He shrugged. "Why don't they just wait until you go back to New York? Less to move, if they still want the furniture and stuff upstairs."

He took another step to me, standing right in front of me, only an arm's length away. I ached to be this close to him and still not be able to touch him. "Because I'm not going back to New York, Syd. I'm staying here at Bribury. I'm going to teach next year too. I'm going to stay for a while. I just agreed to an offer from the dean yesterday."

"Wow, you're sure getting the deals lately," I said. My mind was already whirring with thoughts of how I'd need to map out my classes next year so I could avoid seeing Billy around campus. I'd thought I'd just needed to get through a couple more weeks of knowing the man I loved was on my little campus, and yet so, so far away from me.

"Yeah, I guess," he said. "Actually, I first approached the dean about me staying on, but he was very receptive to the idea."

"Of course he was, you're a great catch for Bribury," I said. I didn't add that he was a great catch for anybody.

"Thanks." He just stared down at me, not saying anything, causing an incredibly awkward silence. At least it seemed awkward to me.

"So, okay. I guess if you don't need me to proofread I'll head out. Congrats on the book again. And, good luck here at Bribury…"

"Wait, Syd." As I walked past him he reached out and took

my arm just above my hand, his touch cool on my flushed skin. "Christ, I am totally messing this up," he said. He chuckled. "I should have *written* what I wanted to say."

I held very still, not daring to guess what he'd planned to say. But hoping. I couldn't stop the hoping. "What did you want to say, Billy?" I said softly.

"I'm staying because of you, Syd. Yes, I found I really loved teaching, but I could do it anywhere. *You're* at Bribury. So *I'm* staying at Bribury." Another deep breath from him, his exhale shaky. "And I'm going to fight like hell to get you back, Sydney O'Brien."

I slid my arm up, still in his hold, until our hands met and I laced my fingers with his. "That's going to be a pretty short battle," I said, squeezing his hand.

He tugged me to him and I fell into his arms. His mouth was on mine and I returned his kiss, two months of pent up frustration finally bursting free.

His arms around me, his taste, the soft breaths he took… All so sweet, all so familiar, all so…mine.

I wrapped my arms around his neck and moved my body closer into his, feeling his already growing erection against me.

He broke away. "Before we go further—and let me just say that we're definitely going to be using the last forty-five minutes we've got with that couch very wisely—I need to tell you something."

"You named your main character after me. You're staying at Bribury. And you've got me back in your arms. What more could you possibly have to tell me?"

He smiled. The smile that had been in the photo I'd printed at the library, and the smile in the picture on his desk, now packed away. The smile I'd loved for years before I ever saw it in person. The smile I would love forever.

"I love you, Syd," he said.

"I love you too, Billy." I ran my hands across his shoulders and buried them in his hair. Yep, my knuckles brushed against the bottom of his neck. Dead-on.

He kissed me again and then broke away, placed his forehead against mine and said, "I'm a writer, I probably should have come up with something more original than just 'I love you, Syd,' right?"

I shook my head. "Don't mess with the classics."

EPILOGUE

⁘

Syd

IT WAS OUR JOB to bring the pizza, so Billy and I were the last to show up at Lucas's apartment for New Year's Eve. Jane, Lily and I had talked about going out, but had ended up wanting to spend the evening together—all of us—where we could just hang out and eat, drink and be merry.

We still lived together for our sophomore year, though in an off-campus apartment instead of the dorms, but with our classes, work, and...relationships, we didn't see each other all that much, so had made a point of doing New Year's Eve together.

I was sure the evening would break up right after midnight, knowing each of the couples would want to be alone to truly ring in the new year together. Because our apartment was only two bedrooms (Lily and Jane shared, since they were used to each other), we'd figured it would make more sense to start at one of the guys' apartments and then split up, instead of at our place.

We couldn't go to Billy's place, being underage students who would be drinking. Which was fine with me. We could do the countdown thing and take off. Go back to his place to be alone, not having to wait for everyone to clear out like

Lucas and Lily would. Although, Stick's apartment was in the same building, just down the hall, so he and Jane wouldn't have much of a journey home.

I guessed the apartment we were partying in tonight used to belong to a friend of Stick's who had been pregnant. When she got married to the baby's father, she'd moved out and Lucas had moved in, his mother well enough to be able to take care of his little brother on her own.

That meant that our apartment would be available later tonight, but I hadn't offered it up to Billy when he'd picked me up. I loved staying at his place, being surrounded by his book collection (even though he mostly read on an ereader), seeing his notes all over the place, even slipping back into my old ways and organizing them for him from time to time. But it wasn't years' worth this time, only a day or two. And they weren't from different scattered ideas, but all pertaining to his current work in progress.

His apartment turned out to be not far from ours, easy walking distance. A quick walk home in the morning to shower and change, say hi to the girls (and sometimes Stick or Lucas if they'd spent the night), and then an easy walk to campus. Jane had her car with her, but seldom took it to campus since the commuter lot was almost as far away from her first class as our apartment was. Mostly she used it to visit Stick on the other side of Schoolport or when we had to get a load of food, though her sporty Corvette wasn't a great grocery-getter.

I spent most nights at Billy's place, but I didn't move in nor did I keep my clothes there, though he'd asked me to both. Just a toothbrush. I thought we both needed some boundaries. Plus, he'd been making noises about looking at a house, using some of the advance he'd received for *Down in Flames*. He'd put his Manhattan apartment into a long-term sublet. It seemed like he was content to stay in Schoolport and at Bribury for the foreseeable future.

A decision I was obviously behind. At least for the next three years, then we'd see where we were at. I was certain we would still be together, and would be for a long time, but I wanted to see what opportunities existed for me after school.

Billy had disclosed our relationship to the dean of his department and to Bribury HR when they'd negotiated his long-term employment. They hadn't been thrilled to know he was dating a student, but they did appreciate his candor, and the fact that he and I hadn't started dating until I was out of his class. As I was no longer his employee, they agreed to, in essence, look the other way where we were concerned.

The reality was, news of his record-breaking deal had just hit the papers when they'd offered him a chance to stay. It was a huge feather in Bribury's cap to have such a renowned author on staff. I thought he could have demanded free sexual access to the entire incoming freshman class and they probably would have said yes.

But he hadn't asked for it. He'd asked only for access to me.

And I honestly think he was prepared to walk if they'd said no.

I'd been worried that teaching as a profession (rather than a just year-long experiment) would cut into Billy's writing now that he was back on track. But that wasn't the case at all.

"About time, I'm starving," Jane said, taking the pizzas from Billy's arms and setting them on the kitchen table. "Booze is on the counter, beer's in the fridge," she said.

"Beer?" I asked Billy. When he nodded, I handed him my coat to put with his while I grabbed two beers from Lucas's refrigerator. By the contents of said fridge, I'd say Lily spent a lot of time here with him and it was stocked with all her favorites.

Billy handed our coats to Lucas, who took them down the hall and into a room. Stick and Billy did the handshake thing. They'd met several times and got along fine, but Billy had certainly not become the third musketeer to Stick and Lucas. Not with his full schedule of classes and writing. And me.

We ate and drank and talked, with the television tuned to Times Square as background noise. At one point I caught Billy watching the show and he turned to me with a smile, both of us remembering last year at this time when he'd sat on the terrace of his parents' apartment and we could hear the city behind us as we FaceTimed.

As we neared midnight, I saw Jane nudging Stick and him giving her a face. Not exactly new behavior for the two of them. "If you don't, I will," Jane hissed at Stick. "Fine," he said back to her.

She left the room and went down the hall, coming back with her backpack in her hands. She pulled out a book and brought it over to where Billy and I sat. I recognized the cover art for *Down in Flames* right away. The newly added "#1 *New York Times* Bestseller" printed large at the top.

"Here," she said, pushing the book at Billy. "I got this for Stick for Christmas. Will you sign it?"

"Uh…yeah, sure, of course," Billy said, somewhat flustered. Jane pulled a Sharpie out of her bag and handed it to him. "Just…to you, Stick?"

As Stick was nodding, Jane said, "Sign it to Patrick."

"Christ, Jane," Stick said under his breath.

Jane only gave him her lethal smile and pointed to the book. "Patrick," she said again to Billy.

Not willing to get in the middle of it, Billy quickly signed the book and handed it back to Jane. She put it back in her bag, thanked Billy and put her bag in the corner of the room, next to some kids' toy that must have belonged to Lucas's little brother.

"Thanks for thinking of the book as a gift for Stick," Billy said to Jane as she grabbed another slice of pizza.

"Sure thing. I don't think he's read it yet, though. I told him *Down in Flames* was about some nutso pyro who burned everything to the ground, just so Stick would start it, but he caught on pretty quickly."

"Ha. Ha," Stick said, glaring at her.

"Well, uh, thanks anyways," Billy said.

"You're welcome," she said. "Besides…it's not the *only* gift I gave him." She looked over her shoulder at Stick who quickly lost the glare, his whole face softening as he returned Jane's grin.

"As always, Fun with Stick and Jane," Lucas said. He and Lily shared a look like indulgent parents of misbehaving children. Then their look turned heated, intimate, and I looked away.

Midnight came and we did the countdown and kisses, keeping it clean. Mostly clean. There were some roaming hands and shuddered breaths in the room, but we all kept it to a minimum.

"Okay," Stick said once the kissing was over. Or, over… for now. "Let's get going," he said to Jane. To Lucas and Lily he added, "Thanks for everything. I'll come over tomorrow and help clean up. Or at least to eat cold pizza."

"Not too early," Lucas said.

We all started to rise, when Lily gave a little chirp. "Oh! Oh, wait. I totally forgot. I wanted to do this right before midnight. Hang on, don't leave yet." She walked down the hall and into what I assumed was Lucas's bedroom.

Jane and I gave each other questioning glances, but it was obvious neither of us knew what Lily was up to. Until she came back into view carrying what looked like envelopes.

"Oh, shit," Jane said. "Lily, we are not—"

"Yes we are," Lily said. It came to me just as she handed me the envelope with my name on the front.

"Oh yeah, I forgot about this," I said. "I can't even remember how the sentence started."

"This time next year I will…" Lily and Jane recited together.

"Right."

"I'll go first," Lily said, ripping open her envelope and pulling out a sheet of paper, which she quickly unfolded.

"We are *not* reading these out loud," Jane said defiantly, but Lily kept going.

"This time next year I will…" She smiled down at the paper. God, she was a beautiful girl. "Still be madly in love with Lucas Kade."

"Oh, gross," Jane exclaimed.

"Lame," I added.

"Boo," from Stick.

Billy just leaned back and spread his arms along the back of the loveseat we shared, keeping quiet.

"Damn straight you are," Lucas said. "And right back at you."

Lily leaned over and kissed him, then looked up at me. "Who's next? Syd?"

"Man, I can't even remember what I put," I said. We'd done this little exercise the night before Montrose had asked me to stay after class, so I was sure there wasn't anything embarrassing about him on my paper. I opened it up and read, "This time next year I will…not be afraid that I don't fit in at Bribury."

Silence. "Who's lame now?" Jane finally said. "Of course you fit in at Bribury. You always did."

I gave a grateful look at Jane who just rolled her eyes at me. "Get a grip," she said.

Billy rubbed on my back. "And? Did it come true?" he asked.

I nodded, then smiled at him. "Yes."

"Good," Stick said. "Still, kind of anticlimactic. Here's hoping you've got a good one, Jane."

"Yeah. No. I think I'll just keep mine private, thank you very much," Jane said.

"Oh, come on," Lily said. "It's just for fun."

"Is it about me?" Stick said, grabbing at her envelope, which Jane held out of his reach.

"Don't be an idiot. We did these last year."

"Yeah, but we danced at your sister's wedding before New Year's."

"But we filled these out before we left for break."

"Oh," Stick said, sitting back in his seat.

"Come on, Jane, read it. We all read ours," I said.

She looked at me and quirked an eyebrow, then ripped open her envelope, looked at her paper and read out loud, "This time next year I will...have finally banged Montrose." There was a tiny gasp from Lily as she looked over at me, trying to gauge my reaction. "And he'll beg for more," Jane finished reading and looked at me with a "happy now?" look.

There was an awkward silence and I could see Stick clench his hands, as if making fists. I felt Billy fidget next to me, and a small "Jesus," escaped under his breath.

But Jane, Jane who had learned a thing or two about diplomacy this past summer on the campaign trail (where she'd helped her father win), while still staying true to herself, stood up, and walked the few steps across the small living room to where Billy and I sat.

"Let me see yours," she said, holding her hand out. I gave her my piece of paper. "Envelope too," she said and I complied. She took a cursory glance at them, not even being able to read them as I'd handed them to her face down.

"Oh, Lily," Jane said, not looking behind her at Lily. "You beautiful, beautiful fool." As Lily was saying "Hey!" Jane continued. "You got Syd's and mine mixed up." She handed me her paper and envelope, clearly labeled "Jane" on the front. "Here Syd, this one was yours. You had mine." She turned and waltzed back to the large, overstuffed chair she shared with Stick. Sitting on his lap, she slung an arm around his shoulders. "See, just a mix-up. All is right with the world."

Everybody smiled and then outright laughed.

"Yeah, that sounds a lot more like it," Billy said as he wrapped an arm around me and pulled me close to his side. "I have definitely begged Syd for more at times."

We all laughed, and the party went on until the three of us girls decided to call it a night.

And go home with the men we loved.

Indeed, all was right with the world.

‿*‿

Try Mara Jacobs's *New York Times* bestselling Worth series

Worth The Weight
Worth The Drive
Worth The Fall
Worth The Effort
Totally Worth Christmas
Worth The Price
Worth The Lies
Worth The Flight
Worth The Burn

Find out more at
www.MaraJacobs.com

Mara Jacobs is the *New York Times* and *USA Today* bestselling author of The Worth Series

After graduating from Michigan State University with a degree in advertising, Mara spent several years working at daily newspapers in Advertising sales and production. This certainly prepared her for the world of deadlines!

Mara writes mysteries with romance, thrillers with romance, and romances with...well, you get it.

Forever a Yooper (someone who hails from Michigan's glorious Upper Peninsula), Mara now splits her time between the U.P. and Las Vegas.

You can find out more about Mara's books at
www.marajacobs.com

Mara loves to hear from readers. Contact her at
mara@marajacobs.com

www.ingramcontent.com/pod-product-compliance
Lightning Source LLC
Chambersburg PA
CBHW031723170626
46808CB00005B/1869